Jack's insp̲i̲r̲a̲t̲i̲o̲n̲ w̲a̲s̲ *W̲o̲n̲d̲e̲r̲s̲ of the World*, one o̲f̲ t̲h̲o̲s̲e̲ e̲d̲u̲c̲a̲t̲i̲o̲n̲a̲l̲ T̲V̲ programs his mother occasionally forced him to watch. This particular program was about the native peoples of the South Pacific, and showed them cooking up huge, slimy worms and eating them at a feast. In this particular culture, worms were considered a delicacy.

"Go figure," quipped Jack.

At first Jack was repulsed by the very sight of people happily chowing down on the creepy crawlers, but as he mulled the scene over in his mind, he began to imagine the reaction he'd get if he served such a dish to his dreaded home economics class. The other kids would positively freak!

CRAWLERS

HOME ICK—O—NOMICS

& Other Tasty Tales

ALLEN B. URY

Tor Kids!
A TOM DOHERTY ASSOCIATES BOOK
NEW YORK

Home Ick-O-Nomics & Other Tasty Tales

Copyright © 1997 by RGA Publishing Group, Inc.

A Tor Book
Published by Tom Doherty Associates, Inc.
175 Fifth Avenue
New York, NY 10010

Tor® is a registered trademark of Tom Doherty Associates, Inc.

ISBN: 0-812-54356-4

First edition: February 1997

Printed in the United States of America

0 9 8 7 6 5 4 3 2 1

For Ed and Carole

Table of Contents

HOME ICK—O—NOMICS

Jack Bolger's eyes widened in shock. His mouth gaped open in fear. His heart raced a mile a minute, and beads of sweat rolled down his ashen face.

The dreadful words on the paper he held in his shaking hands stabbed into his brain like red-hot pokers. He read the words again and again, refusing to believe the horrifying message they contained.

But there was no way around the awful truth. As an eighth-grader at Bowman Junior High School, Jack Bolger was being required to take— *gasp!*—home economics!

"No way!" Jack muttered as he stared at the

paper. "They can't make me take home ec! That's a *girl's* course!"

He immediately ran to his mother and showed her the notice that had just come in the mail.

"Look at this!" he cried, his voice quivering. "They're saying I have to take home economics! There must be some kind of mistake!"

"I don't think so, dear," his mother replied calmly. "I heard that starting this year they want both boys *and* girls to take home ec. After all, everyone needs to know how to run a home, male *or* female. Personally, I think it's a fine idea."

Jack couldn't believe what he was hearing. His own mother—the woman who had brought him into this world, who'd driven him to Little League, mended his soccer uniform, and given him money to go to countless action-adventure movies—was saying that he should take a girl's class!

This isn't my mother, Jack thought, his blood running cold. *She must have been taken over by aliens!*

He immediately ran upstairs to his father's study. There he found his dad working away at his home computer.

"Look at this!" he cried, shoving the notice into his dad's face. "They're making me take home ec! You've got to do something! You've got to make them stop! If you don't, they'll turn me into a—a—a sissy!"

"Nonsense, son," his father replied with a

smile, placing a firm hand on Jack's shoulder. "Home economics is about more than just cooking and cleaning. It's about learning to balance a budget, to manage a household. Besides, there's nothing sissyish about cooking and cleaning. Some of the world's greatest cooks are men."

Jack stumbled back in terror. He couldn't believe his father—the guy who had taught him to hit a baseball, defend himself against bullies, and rack up a dozen bonus lives on his *DeathMatch* video game—was actually defending this sick and twisted decision!

It must be a conspiracy, he told himself. *I once heard Mom and Dad say that they always wanted a girl. Now they're trying to turn me into one!*

For the entire week before the start of school, Jack begged and pleaded with his parents to get him out of the class. But no matter how much he whined and moaned, his folks refused to give in. Besides, they insisted there was nothing they could do. This was school policy, and if he needed a semester of home economics to graduate, then by golly, he'd just have to take the course.

The first day of ninth grade, Jack dragged himself up the school's front steps, his back stooped, his eyes fixed on the ground. He was soon joined by several other boys, each in the same droopy state.

"Did you hear what we have to take this

semester?" groaned Larry Willis, a tall, skinny kid with hair as red as a fire engine. "Home economics."

"I know," moaned Weston LePage, a normally bright and energetic sandy-haired boy who now looked as if he'd just come off a twenty-mile hike through a leech-infested swamp. "I begged my folks to get me out, but they said they couldn't."

"It's a plot," whispered Harold Oates, a chubby fourteen-year-old who was rarely seen without a bag of chocolate-covered peanut butter balls. "The women on the school board want to turn us into—*them.*"

"We ought to protest," Jack insisted. "When it comes time to go to class, we should all refuse."

"A boycott!" Weston agreed.

"A revolt!" Larry chimed in.

"A rebellion!" Harold yelled.

Jack raised his hand, and the other three joined their hands with his.

"Long live men!" he declared.

"A-*men!*" they all shouted in unison.

But when ten o'clock rolled around and it was time for the ninth-grade home economics class to begin, Jack, Larry, Weston, and Harold were all sitting dutifully at their desks, hands folded, feet planted firmly on the floor. These four—as well as every other boy in the class—stared straight ahead. None had the courage to lock eyes with another boy. Each secretly hoped that perhaps his presence would not be noticed by the others.

Better still, each believed that if he just prayed hard enough, he'd simply disappear.

No such luck.

As soon as the bell rang, a thin, stern-faced woman who, rumor had it, was born on Lincoln's Birthday—Lincoln's *actual* birthday, February 12, 1806—stood and addressed the class.

"Welcome to home economics," she said in a voice that sounded like nails grating on a blackboard. "I am Mrs. Boyle, and I want to give a special welcome to all the boys who've joined us this year. I usually don't have the pleasure of seeing so many bright and eager male faces, and I promise you all, this will be a semester you won't forget for the rest of your lives."

Right, Jack thought. *Just like I'll never forget the time I got poison oak at summer camp.*

"Our first project will involve cooking," Mrs. Boyle said, shuffling over to her blackboard. "Each of you will be expected to prepare a dish from scratch, which will then be shared by the rest of the class."

As one, the boys gave a painful groan.

"When you say prepare a dish, you mean, like, make a plate or a bowl?" Wilbur Toddslacker asked with a snicker. "Can it be made of wood?"

"I mean, you will cook food," Mrs. Boyle replied sternly. Jack figured that if the old woman ever cracked a smile, her entire face would probably shatter. "I'm going to pass a card to each of you. It will describe the type of course you are to prepare: appetizer, salad, main dish, or dessert. Then it will be up to you to decide what to make. Is that clear?"

"Crystal clear," said Dana Hellstrom, the pink-cheeked goody-goody who was currently vice president of the student council. She then offered to pass out the cards for Mrs. Boyle, and the shriveled-up teacher agreed.

As Donna moved up and down the rows handing out slips of paper, Jack prayed he'd be assigned a dessert. He knew he could prepare one of those, and if it didn't come out perfect, it would be loaded with enough sugar to at least taste good.

But when he opened his slip, Jack saw, to his horror, that he'd been assigned a main dish.

No! No! This can't be happening! his mind screamed in protest. *Please, have an earthquake swallow me up. Send a flaming meteor crashing into the school. Anything but this!*

Once again, no such luck.

"Now, in preparation for this project, we are going to study basic nutrition," Mrs. Boyle droned on, pointing to a ragged-edged chart showing the four main food groups. "It is very important that as young adults you eat healthy, well-balanced meals. After all, as the old saying goes, 'You are what you eat.' Eat healthy and you'll be healthy. Eat junk and you'll suffer as a result."

Jack grimaced. *No way I could suffer more*

than I'm suffering now, he thought, and immediately he began to plot a way out of this mess.

Jack's inspiration came during *Wonders of the World,* one of those educational TV programs his mother occasionally forced him to watch. This particular program was about the native peoples of the South Pacific, and showed them cooking up huge, slimy worms and eating them at a feast. In this particular culture, worms were considered a delicacy.

"Go figure," quipped Jack.

At first Jack was repulsed by the very sight of people happily chowing down on the creepy crawlers, but as he mulled the scene over in his mind, he began to imagine the reaction he'd get if he served such a dish to his dreaded home economics class. The other kids would positively freak! The girls would probably scream and faint. And old Mrs. Boyle? Heck, she'd probably have a heart attack right there on the spot, and they'd have to cancel the class! Then he and the other boys would at long last be free souls. It was an opportunity too good to pass up.

Unfortunately, a quick tour of his local pet and bait stores failed to produce any of the giant grub worms he'd seen on the cable show. Then he remembered hearing somewhere that in some exotic cultures, people ate french-fried grasshoppers and chocolate-covered ants. Since a chocolate coating would be considered dessertlike, and he'd been assigned a main dish, Jack settled on the grasshoppers.

Fortunately, the overgrown field behind the hardware store on Arthur Avenue was teeming with them this time of year. Armed only with his quick reflexes and a large, empty mayonnaise jar, Jack struck out in search of his prey. Within an hour, he'd captured all the grasshoppers he figured his class could stomach.

Next, a quick trip to the microwave oven rendered his creepy-crawly captives lifeless. And from there it was a short visit to the deep fryer, followed by a generous shower of garlic salt, onion powder, and various other more exotic seasonings.

"Mrs. Boyle," he said to himself, lifting his plate of french-fried grasshoppers off the countertop, "your main dish is served."

The next day, after the students in Mrs. Boyle's class arrived with the dishes that would earn them their first grade, Jack Bolger walked in with his crunchy main course. There were salads, soups, meats, fancy sandwiches, potatoes of every imaginable type, and enough desserts to put half the school in sugar shock for the remainder of the semester. Although a few of the samples were positively grotesque—it was unlikely that anyone was going to make a meal of Harold Oates's peanut butter meatballs—most of the entries actually looked, well, good enough to eat.

One by one, the students stood before the class, presented their culinary creations, then shared them with their classmates. The presentations began with appetizers, moved on to salads, and then came to Jack's category—the main dish.

After several other people offered such things as Hawaiian hamburgers, Cajun meatloaf, and pizza bagels, Jack rose from his seat and carried his delicacy to the head of the classroom.

"What I brought today is considered a real treat in many parts of the world," he announced. "The dish is high in protein, rich in vitamins, and helps agriculture by eliminating local pests."

The other students looked at each other curiously.

With a dramatic flourish, Jack reached down and removed the cover from his tray. "My fellow students, I give you french-fried grasshoppers!"

A deadly silence settled over the room. All around, eyes widened in shock as they gazed upon Jack's lovingly arranged pattern of golden-brown, crispy locusts.

A moment later Dana Hellstrom screamed, and several other girls groaned in disgust.

"Gross," Larry Willis declared, his eyes wide with delight.

"Cool," Weston LePage gasped happily.

Giddy with excitement, Jack turned to see if

Mrs. Boyle had yet died of a heart attack. He was disappointed to see that his teacher was still alive and well and staring at him with a most unamused expression.

"Very creative," she intoned. "Now, perhaps you'd care to show us how to properly eat this delicacy?"

Jack gulped. Did she just say *eat?*

"Well, uh, you just pop 'em in your mouth and chow down," he said with forced levity.

"Please demonstrate," Mrs. Boyle commanded, her eyes locked with his.

All of a sudden, Jack realized that his gag was about to make him, well, *gag.*

"Well? We're waiting," Mrs. Boyle said.

His hand shaking, Jack reached down, picked up one of the two-inch insects by its long, thin legs, raised it to his mouth, and . . .

"Go on Jack. Eat it!" Mrs. Boyle snarled.

Determined not to let her get the best of him, Jack steeled himself, then dropped the awful thing onto his tongue and ever so slowly chewed. As his salivary juices began to interact with the french-fried insect, he detected the pleasant taste of garlic combined with just the right hint of onion and oregano. Steadily, his chewing accelerated as he crunched down on the insect's exoskeleton. *Hmm, not bad.*

All around him, the other kids were staring in openmouthed wonder. It was as if they'd just watched him eat shards of glass or something. Then Jack swallowed and smiled at Mrs. Boyle.

"Try another one," she ordered. "They're awfully small."

Less hesitant this time, Jack grabbed another grasshopper, popped it into his mouth, and chewed it up.

"Actually, they're quite tasty," he said, dabbing his lips with a napkin. "You really should try—"

Just then, he felt his right shoulder give an involuntary twitch. A moment later, his left leg jerked for a brief second.

What's going on? he thought with alarm. *Why do I suddenly feel so . . . jumpy?*

Again, his shoulders twitched, and he suddenly had the irresistible urge to squat on his haunches. A nervous rumble ran through the classroom as Jack, obviously unable to control his actions, began hopping around the front of the room like some oversized bunny rabbit.

And then all of a sudden he felt something irritating in his chest. He stopped, cleared his throat, and coughed up a wad of brown, stinky material that looked suspiciously like chewing tobacco!

The other students twisted their faces in disgust as Jack once again began hopping madly around the room. Then, in an acrobatic display rivaling a circus performer's, he leaped clear across the room—and stuck to the back wall!

Help me! Jack's mind screamed. *Someone, do something!*

But although Jack's mind thought these words, all that managed to come out of his mouth was a high-pitched chirping, like the sound of crickets on a warm summer's night.

Her face still expressionless, Mrs. Boyle stepped forward to once more address her students.

"Let this be a lesson to you all," she said in her rough, scratchy voice. "Be careful what you put in your bodies. Like I told you on the first day of class . . ." In a flash, Jack realized the awful fate he had unknowingly designed for himself, a fate Mrs. Boyle smugly was about to announce. Coldly, she looked at Jack as he hung on the wall, his legs turning thin and bent, his eyes becoming large, black spots on his head. Then she finished her sentence: ". . . you are what you eat!"

THE ZIT OF THE CENTURY

Being fourteen years old, Westin Conroy had suffered his share of pimples. Most of them were the small, pinkish dots barely visible against his otherwise smooth, tan skin. Whenever these would appear, he'd simply make sure to wash his face vigorously before going to bed, and within a day or so they'd disappear.

But lately a few large, more aggressive eruptions had blasted out on Westin's forehead and cheeks. These he recognized as the classic "zits" of teenagehood, and he successfully hid them with the medicated cream his father routinely bought him at the drugstore. As before, they usually cleared up in a day or so.

Westin had known older kids whose faces had

been literally covered with fat, red pimples—
acne, his mother had called the condition—and
he knew that picking at these pus-filled sores
could leave permanent scars. Fortunately, his
own zits had never gotten nearly that bad, and
he suspected that they never would . . . until
he got what he referred to as the "Zit of the
Century."

He first noticed it when he awoke Monday
morning and stumbled sleepily into the bathroom. When he flipped on the light and looked in
the mirror, he initially thought that his eyes
must have been playing tricks on him. There, in
the middle of his forehead, like a big red bull's-
eye, was a reddish bump the size of Mount
Everest.

Actually, it was only about the size of a dime-
sized mosquito bite, but set against Westin's otherwise clean, handsome face, the pimple called
attention to itself like a fifty-foot-high neon sign on
a stretch of open country road.

Westin leaned closer to the mirror and gingerly
rubbed the red lump with his finger. It felt hot and
hard, like a miniature volcano ready to erupt.
Alarmed, he rubbed harder, as if it were an ink
stain that he could erase with the right amount of
pressure.

But the red swelling wouldn't disappear. In fact,
it actually became redder. Feeling sick to his
stomach, Westin ran some hot water for a few

moments, grabbed his soap, lathered up his hands, and carefully rubbed the suds into his forehead. But when he rinsed off, the Zit of the Century was still there in all its crimson glory.

"Oh, great," Westin moaned. "Just what I need. Now everyone at school is going to be staring at Mount Zit, right smack in the center of my forehead."

But Westin was wrong. His friends didn't stare at him. No, instead they pointed at his zit, laughed at it, and made disgusting jokes about it all day long.

"Hey, Wes, whatcha growing, a third eye?" asked Brandon Metcalf, who had been his friend since sixth grade.

"Better stand back, guys. She's gonna blow!" cried Ralph Doberman, who, thanks to his chocolate addiction, had sported a few prize-winning pimples of his own.

"All right, you jerks, cut it out," Westin said as he shoved his books into his locker. "It's just a zit, okay? Everybody gets them, even you guys. It'll go away in a few days."

"You're right, Wes," Ralph agreed. "Everybody gets zits. But that, my friend, is the Grand Pooh-Bah of Pimples!"

Jerry Kazanjian, who sat next to Westin in homeroom, put an arm around his friend's shoulder and drew him aside. "You know, I had a friend who got a zit like that once," Jerry remarked confidentially. "He went to bed with a clear forehead, and the next morning, *poof!* There it was. Just like that monstrosity on your forehead."

"And?" Westin asked cautiously, wondering exactly what Jerry's point was.

"Well, it turned out that it wasn't a zit after all," Jerry replied with a sinister grin. "For two weeks it just kept getting bigger and bigger until one day, when he was washing it—pow! The thing popped." Jerry paused for dramatic effect. "And you'll never guess what came out."

Westin stared at Jerry with a look of dread. "What?" he asked.

"Spiders!" Jerry whispered. "Dozens of tiny baby spiders."

Westin's face twisted as the awful image filled his mind.

"It turned out a spider had bitten my friend while he slept," Jerry went on, encouraged by Westin's obvious disgust. "Then it laid its eggs underneath the skin of his forehead. The eggs fed off the blood in his skin until they matured and hatched."

"Wh-what happened to your friend after that?" Westin stammered.

"He had to be chained up in a mental hospital for six months," Jerry said sadly. "Even now he has to go to a special school for kids who never talk. It seems the experience scared him so much, he hasn't uttered a single word since."

After listening to Jerry's story, everyone fell silent. Then Ralph burst out laughing. "Oh, right, tell us another one!" he jeered. "That story is soooo lame!"

"It's true!" Jerry insisted, acting offended.

"Don't listen to him, Wes," Ralph advised. "I've heard that story—or some version of it, anyway—dozens of times. It always happens to someone's friend or a friend of a friend, but the truth is, it never really happened at all. It's just one of those modern tall tales, like that story about the escaped mental patient with the hook for a hand that people tell around campfires."

Westin knew the story Ralph was talking about and realized that he was just being made a fool of. After all, what kind of a dork did Jerry think he was?

"So who *was* this friend you're talking about, anyway?" he challenged Jerry. "What's this guy's name?"

"I can't tell you," Jerry said, lowering his eyes. "I've been sworn to secrecy."

"Yeah, right, and I work for the CIA," Brandon said sarcastically. Then he turned to face Westin. "Ralph's right. It's just a zit. Until it goes away, just wear a baseball cap real low on your head."

Westin decided that wasn't such a bad idea, and for the rest of the day he managed to distract attention away from his zit by borrowing a spare cap from Ralph. Still, when he got home and dared to check in the bathroom mirror, the Zit of the Century had grown even bigger. Now, it looked like the Zit of the Millennium! What the heck was he supposed to do, wear a hat for the rest of his life?

"I think I should see a skin doctor," he told his mother the minute she arrived home from work. "I want someone to take a look at this thing." He pointed to the horror that was spreading across his forehead.

Westin's mother bent down to better examine the gross spot. "Son, that is one major zit," she said, sounding oddly proud. "Whatever you do, don't pick at it. It could leave a permanent scar, you know."

"But I don't think it's just a pimple," Westin insisted.

"Well, what else do you think it is?" his mother asked with genuine curiosity.

Westin paused for a moment, uncertain as to how best to break the news. "I think it might be a . . ."

"A what?" his mother asked impatiently.

"Well, I think it might be some kind of spider's nest."

For a moment his mother said nothing, struggling to maintain a straight face. Then she burst out laughing. "Wait, don't tell me—someone told you the one about the girl who fell asleep on the beach and woke up with a bite on her cheek!" She shook her head helplessly. "Come on, Westin. That story's even older than *I* am!"

"Jerry said it happened to this guy he knows," Westin corrected her. "And it wasn't at the beach, it was while he was in bed."

"In bed or on the beach—it's the same old silly story people tell to gross other people out," his mother said, heading for the kitchen. "I heard it myself when I was your age. Now, stop worrying. All you have is a very large pimple. No creepy little insects are going to pop out of it. I promise."

As much as Westin wanted to believe his mother, he couldn't find any way to reassure himself that she was telling the truth. That night he was plagued by nightmares about being overrun by hordes of spiders and beetles and hissing cockroaches. Unfortunately, the one dream he had that wasn't filled with bugs was just as bad. It involved a seemingly ordinary pimple on his left cheek that grew and grew until it covered his entire face. When it finally popped, his whole head was sucked into the gooey crater it had left behind.

The next morning, Westin hurried into the bathroom to examine his forehead, still shaking from these freakish images. What he saw made him wish he was still asleep. The monstrous pimple was bigger than ever, and when Westin squinted closely at it, he thought he could see something moving around—*inside!*

Now Westin was truly scared. He remembered once seeing a movie on cable TV about a space alien that had planted its egg right inside an astronaut's chest, and the resulting baby burst out of the poor man's rib cage. *Could that be happening to me?* Westin wondered, gulping back his terror. *Could something be growing inside my head?*

His heart pounding, Westin raced into his parents' bedroom across the hall and forced them to inspect the nasty eruption.

"You're right, Wes. I think you *should* see a doctor about that," his father said, after examining the huge red bump on his son's head. "It could be a boil, for all we know."

"What's a boil?" Westin asked nervously.

"It's like a pimple, only more serious," his father explained. "It's caused by staph bacteria. Yes, I think we should make an appointment for you right away."

Westin went to school that morning wearing a large bandage over his ever-growing zit. He couldn't even fit Ralph's baseball cap over it now, and besides, it hurt far too much. Whenever his friends asked him what was underneath the bandage, he explained that he had been accidentally hit by a baseball. Finally, fifteen minutes after school had ended and his mother had picked him up at the front entrance, they were sitting in the office of Dr. George Lauber, a dermatologist.

"Well, Westin, I haven't seen you since you had that nasty case of poison ivy!" Dr. Lauber said, chuckling as he entered the examining room. "So, son, what can I do for you today?"

Westin slowly removed the bandage from his forehead, and Dr. Lauber's normally sunny expression suddenly turned to one of shock. He fumbled for his examining light, peered through the magnifying eyepiece, and gradually approached the zit like an insect specialist cautiously approaching some endangered species.

"My, my, my," Dr. Lauber mumbled, examining the zit from all angles. "When did you get *this*?"

"Only two days ago," Westin informed him. "My dad thinks it might be some kind of boil thing."

"Well, it's like no boil I've ever seen," Dr. Lauber said, stepping back and stroking his graying beard. "But just to be certain, I think we should lance it."

Westin didn't like the sound of that, and he sure didn't like the look of the small, wickedly sharp instrument that Dr. Lauber now clutched in his latex-gloved hand.

"Now, I'm just going to make a small surgical incision to drain the pus," Dr. Lauber explained. "Then I'll put you on some antibiotics to fight the infection."

"Will it hurt?" Westin asked, closing his eyes in

a quick prayer as Dr. Lauber produced a syringe with a needle that looked to be about as long as his arm.

"Hurt?" Dr. Lauber echoed, bending down and dabbing the area around the zit with alcohol. "No, no, it won't hurt *me* a bit." He chuckled at his joke, then gently touched the point of the needle to the base of the zit. "That should numb the area in just a moment. Then you won't feel a thing."

Westin struggled to hold himself still.

"Don't move, this should only take—" Dr. Lauber suddenly stopped short.

"What is it?" Westin's mother asked in alarm.

"I don't believe this!" the doctor gasped, staggering backward.

The next moment, Westin felt a horribly painful, burning sensation between his eyes, as if someone had stuck his forehead with a red-hot poker. He screamed as the pain intensified despite the shot the doctor had given him earlier to numb the area.

Instinctively raising his hands to his head, Westin felt something hot and sticky on his palms—and when he pulled them down for a look, he nearly fainted in shock. His hands were coated with a mixture of blood and some thick, greenish-yellow substance.

Terrified, Westin leaped from the chair and rushed over to a nearby mirror. What he saw made him want to scream, but his mouth froze in horror.

There, directly in the center of his forehead, was a gaping hole about two inches in diameter, and inside the hole was some kind of large, scaly worm or small, coiled snake. Transfixed, Westin watched as the squirming creature raised its pointed head to reveal two oversized, reddish eyes. Then, as if realizing that someone had just discovered it, the creature leaped from its fleshy "cocoon" like a taut metal spring.

Westin's mother shrieked like a banshee as the bizarre creature landed in the sink with a distinct *splat*. It thrashed about for a second or two, then appeared to spot the nearby drain and squirmed toward it.

"No!" Dr. Lauber shouted, lunging for the sink and shoving Westin roughly out of the way in the process. "We have to save it somehow!"

But the doctor was too late. The wormy creature had slithered completely into the drain and was now beyond reach.

Dr. Lauber collapsed against the counter, his skin as white as his latex gloves.

"What *was* that?" Westin's mother asked, her hand pressed over her heart.

Before the doctor could reply, Westin felt his legs grow suddenly weak and his head seem lighter. The next moment, the world around him began to spin, and he crashed to the floor.

* * *

That night Westin stayed in the hospital, and
the next day he was sent home to recuperate.
The doctors had treated his head wound with
numerous medicines, then closed it with twelve
stitches. Dr. Lauber said there would most likely
be a scar when the wound healed, but it would
be minimal. He strongly suggested that Westin
tell anyone who was curious that it was just a
"*very* bad bug bite."

The following Saturday afternoon, Westin's
friends Ralph, Brandon, and Jerry gathered
around his bed to examine the stitches and talk to
him about his odd affliction.

"Did the doctors have *any* idea what that thing
was?" Ralph asked, relishing the idea of a
strange, alien organism living right here in their
neighborhood.

"Not really," Westin admitted. "They think it
was probably some kind of roundworm that got
mutated from pesticides or something. They've
sent a bulletin out to all the doctors around town
to keep an eye out for similar cases."

"I wonder where you picked it up," Brandon said.

"I guess it could have been anywhere," Westin
replied. "Maybe even right here in this room."

The boys looked nervously around them.

"I guess my story about spider eggs wasn't so far
off after all," Jerry joked, with forced humor.
"Just one thing bothers me. If that thing that

came out of your forehead came from an egg, then it was a baby, right? And if it was a baby, then what I want to know is, where's the thing's mother?"

Again, the boys looked around fearfully. Then, as one, they slowly backed toward the doorway.

"Nice seeing ya, Wes, old boy," Ralph said with a weak little wave.

"Get better soon," Brandon added, tripping over his own feet in his haste.

"See you at school, pal," Jerry mumbled.

Together the three boys bolted out the door, ran down the stairs, and disappeared out of the house.

Westin sighed and pulled the covers up to his chin. He tried to get comfortable, but couldn't help but wonder if another wormthing might still be lurking somewhere in his bedroom . . . watching . . . waiting . . . looking for another perfect chance to attack him.

For several minutes, Westin lay there silently, listening to his own quickening breathing. Feeling odd little twitches all over his face, he couldn't help but feel that the thing had already laid more eggs. But it was probably just his imagination, right?

Deciding to go to the bathroom for a drink of water, he thrust off the covers and stood up, stumbled down the hall, snapped on the light, and paused when he saw something weird in the bathroom mirror. Then he burst out with hysterical laughter. Boy, did he have one heck of an imagination! Now he wasn't just feeling things, he was seeing things, too—actually, *three* things, to be exact.

Mesmerized by what he saw in the mirror, Westin fixed his eyes on the three tiny red spots that had appeared on his chin. They looked a lot like pimples, but these pimples were growing . . . right before his eyes!

THE COLLECTION

 e careful, honey," Lorraine's mom advised
as her fourteen-year-old daughter prepared to
leave the house. "Remember, there's a lot of
poison ivy growing in those woods. You don't want
to spend the next week covered in calamine
lotion."

"I'll be fine, Mom," Lorraine Stevenson said confidently. "I know how to dress for the woods.
Nothing's going to touch me." Picking up her butterfly net and collection jar, she headed for the front
door. "I'll be back by suppertime," she called over
her shoulder. "We're having hamburgers, right?"

"Your Sunday night favorite," Mrs. Stevenson
replied with a smile, which Lorraine didn't see.
She'd already given her mom a backward wave and

had headed out of the house for the familiar ten-block trek to the Jasper Woods Forest Preserve.

An eighth grader at the Hyneck Junior High in Ann Arbor, Michigan, Lorraine Stevenson was a bright, attractive, dark-haired girl with a lifelong fascination with insects. In fact, she'd been an avid bug collector since she was only seven years old, and had built up one of the most extensive collections of butterflies, moths, dragonflies, beetles, roaches, and spiders in her entire school.

Naturally, when the school held its annual science fair, Lorraine chose the field of entomology—the study of insects—and had won first prize both years that she'd competed. This year, she planned to enter her insect display once again, and she hoped to add a very special specimen that would once more clinch her the blue ribbon.

Earlier that month, word had spread like wildfire among entomologists in the area that a Ballantine monarch, a rare and exotic butterfly, had been spotted in the area. Several additional sightings had confirmed the insect's presence, although an actual specimen had yet to be captured.

Lorraine hoped that she would be the first person to get her hands on an actual Ballantine monarch, and had developed a very simple yet clever plan. She knew that all monarch butterflies love milkweed, a plant common throughout the Midwest. So she collected several milkweed plants, boiled them down, and created a pungent "perfume" that she carried with her for bait as she made her way toward Jasper Woods. Yes, by making *herself* as irresistible to the butterfly as the smell of meat is to a dog, Lorraine felt sure that the Ballantine monarch would be hers in no time.

Reeking with the milkweed potion she'd dabbed behind her ears and slathered on her face after leaving the house, Lorraine entered Jasper Woods and followed a path that took her about a quarter of a mile into the wooded preserve. There, in a large, open field often visited by monarch butterflies at this time of year, she set down her collection jar and opened the small, wax-lined box that held the rest of the milkweed extract.

You can never have too much bait when you're trying to capture a prize like the Ballantine monarch, she thought as she stood back and waited patiently for the coveted insect to appear.

And over the next hour or so, dozens of monarchs did appear to sniff at Lorraine, but unfortunately, none had the distinct gold lining around their wings unique to the Ballantine. Then, at about five o'clock, just when she was convinced the elusive insect would not rear its beautiful head, lo and behold, a monarch butterfly with a thin stripe of yellow-gold on its wing tips fluttered down to get a whiff of her milkweed concoction.

Her heart beating as wildly as an insect's wings, Lorraine gripped the handle of her butterfly net and carefully approached her unsuspecting prey. Slowly, very slowly, she crept forward and . . .

"Gotcha!" she cried as she swiped the net down upon the Ballantine, quickly twisting the netting to prevent its escape. Then she carefully transferred the rare and beautiful creature into a specimen jar. "You're mine!" she exclaimed proudly.

As if in protest, the captured monarch beat its wings frantically, like it was trying to fly through the glass. Lorraine was filled with awe and a touch of sadness for her little prisoner. It was a shame that such a fragile, beautiful creature had to die. But if she didn't kill it, there'd be no way to mount it for her science project.

A girl's gotta do what a girl's gotta do, she thought, gathering up her equipment and starting back on the path for home. *Besides, it's all in the name of science, right?*

She was halfway down the path when the smell hit her. What was it? Burgers? A steak? Whatever it was, it was barbecued, and it smelled delicious enough to make her mouth water.

Her stomach growling, Lorraine soon turned off the path in the direction of the irresistible aroma. Although growing more and more obsessed with the smell, she did manage to keep her eyes peeled for poison ivy as she pressed ahead through the light, woodsy undergrowth.

"I've got to at least *see* those hamburgers," she

mumbled to herself. "Maybe whoever's cooking them will even let me have one!"

Lorraine was deep into the woods when it suddenly occurred to her that there were no public picnic areas in the direction she was headed. Although she thought this strange, she figured that maybe the campers had brought some kind of portable barbecue. Shrugging off any doubts, and overwhelmed by the need to taste the sizzling beef, Lorraine stumbled into a small, dimly lit clearing.

But instead of finding a cookout in progress, Lorraine was surprised to see what looked like two young children with their backs turned toward her. They were standing over a shoe-box-sized device covered with air vents. Apparently the irresistible aroma was coming from this odd little machine.

"What do you have in there?" Lorraine asked, forcing a smile. "It smells absolutely *delicious*!"

Seemingly startled, the two children turned to face her. But when Lorraine saw their faces, she realized these weren't children at all—at least, not *human* children.

Their skin leathery gray, their eyes huge and segmented like a fly's, these creatures had insect-like pincers for mouths and clawlike hooks covered with thick, coarse hairs for hands.

Terrified out of her mind, Lorraine screamed. Although both of the monstrous creatures were momentarily shocked by the loud, high-pitched sound, one of them recovered in time to raise a glowing, whiplike device and snap it in her direction. The edge of the whip struck Lorraine in the lower right arm, causing a sharp, painful sting. Screeching even louder, she suddenly felt every muscle in her body go limp. Then her eyes rolled back in her head, and she dropped to the leaf-covered ground, unconscious.

Lorraine slowly opened her eyes and shook her head, as if trying to shake out a bad dream. The pursuit of the phantom cookout, her encounter with the buglike children, the sting from the strange glowing whip—it all seemed too incredible to have been real.

But when she opened her eyes and looked around, Lorraine realized that her experience had been all *too* real. She was in a stark white room, lying on some kind of metal examining table, her arms, legs, and neck clamped firmly in place. Above her, a strange instrument was scanning her body with dozens of hair-thin beams of ruby-red light. At the far end of the room stood the two buglike children, their attention fixed on a bank of bizarre, light-covered instrument panels. Their conversation, though difficult to understand, was clearly about her.

"The long-haired biped responded as predicted," one of the creatures was saying. His clawlike mouth didn't actually move, but Lorraine clearly heard his words deep within her mind.

"We are lucky it responded readily to the olfactory bait and fell right into our trap," the other responded. "Now we are ready to—"

"Hey, what's going on here?" Lorraine shouted, struggling vainly against her restraints. "I don't know what planet you're from, but I demand that you let me go immediately!"

The two small creatures turned their huge, bug-like eyes toward Lorraine, their mouths twitching nervously.

"It's conscious," the first creature stated.

"Not for long," its companion replied.

"What do you want?" Lorraine pleaded as tears welled up in her eyes. "Why are you doing this to me?"

The two bug creatures shuffled forward on their thin, spindly legs. Then they took a position on either side of the examining table.

"Notice the fine dark hair," the first creature said, running one of its claws over Lorraine's head. "The smooth, fleshy skin. The small eyes placed close together at the front of the head."

"It will make a fine addition to our collection," the second creature hissed as it turned around and pressed a button on the wall.

A moment later, a section of the wall slid back. Now Lorraine could see another room beyond this one. It was filled with a dozen large glass cylinders.

In each, illuminated by a small overhead light, was an alien creature of some kind, suspended in a clear gel.

Lorraine gasped. For someone who'd collected insects most of her life, the purpose of this chamber was terrifyingly clear. These beings—some reptilian, some birdlike, some covered with oddly colored fur—were animal specimens obviously taken from throughout the galaxy. It was also painfully obvious to Lorraine that she was to join this group as a representative of the Homo sapiens species. Yet how could they be so cruel as to collect a human? Her collecting of insects was one thing, but collecting *humans*—that was something else!

"This one will be our finest specimen," the first bug creature declared. "Now we will win the science competition for sure!"

"What?" Lorraine cried. "You're entering me in some kind of interplanetary science fair? No way!"

Again she fought frantically against her bonds, but the metal clamps were locked tight and held her firmly in place.

"The human is out of control," the second creature said calmly. "Let's terminate her. She's too dangerous alive."

Nodding its agreement, the first creature produced a pistol-like device at the end of which was a very long hypodermic needle.

Now, Lorraine considered herself a pretty brave

young woman. She had once jumped headfirst off a twenty-foot-high diving board. She'd ridden on her big cousin Tony's motorcycle. She'd even tried sushi. But there was one thing that terrified Lorraine beyond all reason, and that was needles.

Needless to say, the sight of this seven-inch monster threw her into a state of panic that, on a scale of one to ten, was clearly a twelve. Her eyes bugged wide, her face twisted beyond all description, and she let out a shriek so high-pitched that a good part of it was audible only to dogs.

The aliens, who had been violently startled when Lorraine had screamed back in the woods, were now twice as shaken by this outburst. In fact, the alien holding the hypodermic needle was so shocked that it dropped the evil-looking device, turned away, and slapped its claws over the thin slits on each side of its bulbous head, obviously trying to shield its version of ears.

The creature's partner was likewise sent into fits of fear and panic. Its confusion grew even worse as Lorraine continued to scream her lungs out.

"Don't touch me!" she shrieked. "Help me! Somebody, help me!"

"Stop that, you despicable creature!" cried the first alien. "That sound! I can't stand it!"

"It hurts!" moaned the second alien, dropping to its knees. "We must make it stop that beastly noise!"

"Let me go!" Lorraine howled, noting that the

louder she screamed, the more discomfort she caused her captors. "Let me go! Let me go! Let me go!"

"*Let it go!*" cried the second space creature. "That horrible biped is killing me!"

Diving for a nearby control panel, the other alien quickly ran its claws over the odd, extra-terrestrial buttons, and a moment later the clamps that held Lorraine in place sprang free. Still screaming, she prepared to bolt upright and make her escape, but before she could, she was hit square in the chest by a brilliant beam of light emanating from the instrument above her.

Seconds later, Lorraine found herself lying faceup on the cool forest ground. Above her, now about twenty feet away, was a dull-gray saucer-shaped craft about thirty feet in diameter. The bright white beam of light, which was still shining on her, suddenly retracted into the smooth under-side of the ship, and almost within that same instant, the spacecraft shot straight up into the air with nothing but a whispery *whoosh*. Before Lorraine could even blink, it had completely vanished from sight.

Feeling faint, Lorraine stayed put for a good five minutes, collecting her strength and trying to convince herself that, yes, she *had* just escaped from two very unfriendly extraterrestrials. Then, noticing that the sky overhead was growing darker, she weakly raised her left wrist and

glanced at her watch. It was 6:57 p.m. Her parents were probably worried sick about her.

Sitting up with a start, she found her butterfly net and collection jar—with the Ballantine
monarch still inside—lying on the ground nearby.
From the weak fluttering of its wings, she could
see that the beautiful creature was still alive . . .
barely.

"Don't worry, Mr. Ballantine, you're gonna be
just fine," she cooed to the frightened monarch.
Then she quickly unscrewed the jar and turned
the container upside down. It took two or three
sharp shakes to get the butterfly to move, but a
few seconds later the exotic insect was free and
flitting happily around her head.

"Go on! Get out of here!" Lorraine cried, waving
a hand through the air. "You're free! Go enjoy
your life!"

As if understanding her, the butterfly flew off
into the nearby trees, where it disappeared from
sight.

At that year's science fair, Lorraine Stevenson
surprised everyone by *not* entering another insect
collection. Instead, she presented a research project entitled, "UFOs: FACT OR FANTASY?" She
devoted much of her report to so-called alien
abductions, concluding that the phenomenon was
all too real.

Although her report was well written and, as

one judge put it, "quite passionate," Lorraine did not win a prize in the competition. Unfortunately all of the judges agreed that the project lacked "any scientific validity whatsoever."

That night, standing out on her stoop and staring up at the stars, Lorraine realized she didn't care that she had lost. Instead, she wondered if some other poor soul had been selected to take her place in the aliens' "collection." Then she had an even more frightening thought: *What if the aliens decided to come back for her . . . and what if, next time, they were smart enough to bring earplugs!*

TOGETHER FOREVER

I know what "cool" is. Skateboards are cool. Staying up 'til midnight watching horror videos is cool. Hawaiian pizza is cool. And snakes—they're *definitely* cool.

Although they don't have any legs, snakes can catch even fast animals, like field mice, who do have legs. They can eat prey bigger than their own heads. They can shed their own skins. And, best of all, most girls freak when they see them. Now that is *ultracool*.

Needless to say, I've wanted a snake for about as long as I can remember, but my sister Tabitha made such a big stink every time I brought up the subject that Mom and Dad said it would be better if I chose a different kind of pet. That was totally unfair. I mean, Tabitha got the hamster *she* wanted. Why couldn't I have the snake *I* wanted?

Fortunately, that's all over now. I got my snake. My uncle Albert gave me a rare—and valuable— Mekong python from Southeast Asia for my thirteenth birthday. He bought it for me while visiting the Far East on business a few weeks ago.

"You know, David, the natives in the village where I bought your snake say that the Mekong python has magical powers," Uncle Albert said. "And according to the villagers, the snake uses its powers to protect its owner from evil."

I looked at my coiled companion and just couldn't see how an eighteen-inch snake could protect me, even if it tried. When I questioned Uncle Albert about this, he just smiled. "Give your little snake some time, David," he said. "You see, a python continues to grow throughout its entire life. Yours will, too."

I put my snake in a shoe box, which I had punched with a pencil to make air holes. Then I started thinking up names for my new pal. I considered famous names like Elvis, plain names like Arnold, and fancy names like Jean-Luc. Then I finally decided on Shaquille after Shaquille O'Neal. He's one of the coolest basketball players I've ever seen, and the way he always slithers around other players on the court reminds me of a snake. Borrowing Shaquille's name, and later his nickname,

Shaq, was a great idea, I thought, and so did my uncle.

Anyway, the next day, I used my allowance to buy Shaq a proper terrarium with all the trimmings: cedar shavings, rocks, a twisted log, phony jungle vines, a water bowl, and a heater. I also bought him food.

"Pythons Shaq's age usually eat only worms and large bugs, like beetles," the man at the pet store told me. Then he proceeded to sell me a variety of gross "snake eats" for two bucks. "I gotta warn you, though," he went on. "You're getting away cheap for now. I've heard of his kind before, and pretty soon that snake of yours will be eating you out of house and home."

I wanted to ask him what he meant by that, but Shaq was really squirming around in his shoe box, so I left.

When I got Shaq home, I put him right into his new terrarium and prepared his feast. "Chow time!" I cried as I dumped a half-dozen clicking beetles and a tangled mess of squirming night crawlers into the tank.

As though he hadn't eaten in days, Shaq attacked the helpless bugs. I watched, completely fascinated as he first snared a bug with his mouth, coiled his body around his prey, then squeezed until the insect's shell cracked like a pistachio nut. It was really disgusting. The poor beetle's legs were still kicking as Shaq swallowed it whole.

After he'd finished eating the bug, I looked at my watch. The entire process had taken less than two minutes. But my stomach was doing flip-flops for a few hours.

By nightfall all the beetles were gone, as were each and every night crawler. Shaquille had curled up in a corner of his terrarium to slowly digest his supper while I sat on the end of my bed admiring my reptile the same way an art student might study a fine painting. I mean, when I think about it, nature designed a near-perfect creature when it came up with the snake. Simple in form, a snake can capture and devour animals that are, at first glance, faster, stronger, and even larger than it is. You have to admire a creature like that. And as I sat there watching Shaq digest his meal, I sure did admire him.

After two weeks, Shaq grew from about one and a half feet to *three* feet long, exactly doubling his size. And his appetite grew right along with him. In fact I had to buy a bag of "snake eats" every day for eight days just to keep up with him. Whew! I had no idea that owning a snake could be so expensive.

Anyway, finally it was clear that Shaq was no longer a baby, and he needed to graduate from bugs and worms to something more "adult"—like baby mice. The guy at the pet store sold me a bunch of the little guys, which he called "pinkies" because they were so young they still hadn't grown white fur over their soft pink skins.

"Start out with one," the pet store man advised. "And see how your snake takes to it."

So I started out with a single pinkie, and Shaq not only took to it, he grabbed it like it was a piece of gold. Within seconds he had wrapped himself around it, strangled it, and gulped the lifeless body down whole. I was grossed out . . . but also fascinated.

The next day I gave Shaq another pinkie, and by the end of the week he was up to three pinkies a day. That's when I decided to give him a full-grown mouse.

Trembling as much as the rodent was, I dropped the wiggling mouse into Shaq's cage. Immediately the poor thing started running around, pawing at the glass, and its white whiskers quivered like antennae, trying to locate some means of escape.

At the opposite end of the cage, Shaq slowly uncoiled himself, his brown eyes locking firmly onto his target. Then, moving with silent stealth, he slid across the tank's cedar-covered floor until he was within three inches of his victim. He paused for a moment, his forked tongue stabbing the air. Then, picking up the mouse's scent—which I figured smelled like pizza or a cheeseburger would to me—he lunged with lightning speed and snared the mouse's head between his powerful jaws.

It was all over in about a minute, and even
before the mouse's body had a chance to get cold,
Shaq's powerful throat muscles had swallowed it
whole. I almost got sick to my stomach, seeing the
huge bulge in the middle of Shaq's tubular body, a
bulge that lasted a couple of days while his reptilian juices digested his meal.

"This is Shaquille, a rare Mekong python from
Southeast Asia," I told my spellbound science
classmates as I held up Shaq's head. The rest of
his body, which was now six feet long, was draped
around my shoulders. "He weighs twenty-two
pounds and lives in a forty-gallon tank in my
bedroom."

As Shaq coiled himself around my neck, I felt his
muscles instinctively tightening. Some people
might say that this is just normal constrictor
behavior, but I have come to believe that it is a
genuine sign of affection. You see, I take very good
care of my snake.

"Pythons are nonpoisonous snakes of the boa
family and are found chiefly in Asia, Africa, and
Australia," I continued, having memorized several
articles on snakes that I found on my computer's
CD-ROM encyclopedia. "Many pythons grow up to
twenty feet in length. The royal python, one of the
largest snakes in the world, can grow as long as
thirty feet."

I smiled as I heard the class give a collective

gasp of astonishment. And Shaq, although he has no ears and couldn't have heard the class's reaction, nonetheless raised his fist-sized head as if to acknowledge his own supreme greatness.

In the middle of the room, a hand went up. It belonged to Louis Gillespie, a chubby, dark-haired kid who's famous for his industrial-sized, eight-course lunches.

"What's he eat?" Louie asked eagerly, as if he wanted to compare diets.

"Right now he eats rats," I answered, delighted that at least half the girls in the class scrunched up their faces and made noises of disgust. "But as he keeps growing," I went on, having a ball freaking everyone out, "he may have to move on to something larger."

"Like what?" some kid called from the back of the room.

"I'm not sure," I admitted. "Any volunteers?"

Nervous laughter rippled through the classroom. Then, not missing a beat, I swiveled my body so that Shaq's head was turned directly toward Loreli Kramer, easily the most high-strung girl in the seventh grade. As expected, Loreli got one good close-up of Shaq and screamed her head off.

Our teacher, Ms. Benson, immediately jumped to her feet before everyone stampeded out of the classroom.

"All right, David, that's quite enough," she said

sternly. "Thank you very much for that . . . uh . . . interesting report."

I gave a slight bow, then took Shaq over to the large Styrofoam cooler I had used to bring him to school. As I crossed the room, I noticed that every eye in the classroom was still glued to me, like I was some kind of celebrity or something.

And in a way, I guess that's what I'd become. Thanks to Shaq, I was—for the first time in my life—the absolute coolest kid in my entire class. And that was *real* cool with me.

Later that afternoon, I was crossing the school yard toward the school buses when Brad Bradshaw, who wasn't in my science class, shouted over to me.

"Hey, Taite!" he called. "Whatcha got in the cooler?"

Before I knew what was happening, Brad and his two buddies, Jason Kroger and Lenny Blatz, had surrounded me. It had been a while since those three bullies had given me any trouble, but now it looked like my luck was about to take a turn for the worse.

"Nothing you'd be interested in," I said nonchalantly, trying my best to avoid eye contact.

"That's *your* opinion," Brad sneered, reaching for the cooler lid. "Let's see what ya got."

"Yeah, maybe he's got drinks," Lenny said stupidly. "I hope so. I'm sure thirsty."

"I wouldn't touch that if I were you," I warned Brad, sidestepping away.

"Shut up and open the cooler," Brad demanded. "Or maybe I'll just do it myself." And with that, he grabbed the lid and yanked it off. "What the—?" he gasped, stumbling back in terror as Shaq's head rose out of the cooler, ready to strike.

"Careful, Brad, he's poisonous," I said, lying through my teeth.

As if on cue, Shaq snapped his head toward Brad in a hunting move he usually reserved for big, hairy rats. Then, like a proud father, I watched as my "son" scared the heck out of my would-be attackers.

Holding nothing back, Brad let out a scream that no self-respecting bully should ever allow out of his mouth. Then he spun on his heels and bolted away like a dog with his tail between his legs.

"I'm outta here!" Jason yelled, following hot on his leader's heels.

"Wait for me!" cried Lenny, racing to catch up.

"Good boy, Shaq," I said soothingly, petting my python's cool, scaly head. Then, returning him to the cooler and replacing the lid, I remembered Uncle Albert's story about how Mekong pythons protect their owners. "Well, Shaq, old buddy, it looks like you're doing your job well. Yup, you and I are going to be together forever, pal. And to show you how much you mean to me, I'm going to give you a nice, fat reward."

* * *

"Mom!" my sister Tabitha screeched. "David stole my hamster!"

"Did not!" I shouted back.

"Did, too!"

"Did not!"

"You stole my hamster and fed it to your big, stupid snake!" Tabitha cried.

"Oh, yeah?" I countered, folding my arms across my chest. "Prove it."

"Fine," she said with a sneer. "I'll cut open your snake and look inside its big, fat stomach!"

"Touch Shaq and he'll eat *you!*" I warned her.

That shut Tabitha up fast, and for a second it looked like she almost believed me. And no wonder—Shaq was now over six feet long, and as big around as my thigh. In fact, I had to get a job mowing lawns just to help pay for all the rats he was eating—about ten a week! Anyway, of course I'd "accidentally" dropped Tabitha's hamster in Shaq's tank, but I sort of had to. After all, I'd promised him something juicy after he'd saved me from those bullies.

"David, did you feed your sister's hamster to your snake?" my mother asked sternly.

"Of course not," I told her with amazing innocence.

"He's lying, Mom," Tabitha said, her eyes boring hatred into me.

"You'd better be telling the truth, young man,"

my mom warned me. "If I ever find you feeding anything but rats to that ... *thing* of yours, he's going straight to the zoo. He belongs there anyway."

"If I'm lying, Tabitha can feed *me* to Shaq," I said confidently, looking at my little squirt of a sister. For some reason I shuddered as I had this really weird thought: *Lucky for me snakes can't hear.*

Over the next two weeks, Shaq had a tremendous growth spurt. He was now fifteen feet long, and had an appetite that was starting to scare me. I didn't let Shaq know this, but I was beginning to think my mom was right. Maybe he did belong in the zoo. He certainly didn't belong in my bedroom anymore—or, rather, he didn't *fit* in there anymore. In fact, my dad and I had to move him into a chicken-wire cage we set up in the garage. But I was already beginning to suspect that he'd outgrow even that in a few weeks' time. As it turned out, it happened sooner than that.

One day, as I headed into the garage with a whole barrelful of rats—Dad was now helping me pay for Shaq's food until we worked something out—I saw, to my horror, that Shaq was gone.

They took him to the zoo! I thought, feeling both upset and relieved. *They could have at least given me a chance to say good-bye!*

I was working up to a good fit of outrage when I noticed that part of Shaq's chicken-wire cage had come loose, creating a hole big enough for him to have slithered through. And then I knew the truth: Shaq was at large, and he was probably very hungry.

"Shaq!" I called, frantically looking around the dimly lit garage. "Shaquille! Where are you?"

And then I realized that, being deaf—on top of being a big, dumb snake—Shaq wasn't exactly going to come slithering into my waiting arms. I also realized that despite his size, Shaq could be hiding just about anywhere.

I opened the barrel of live rats—that truly made my skin crawl—figuring that while I looked for him, Shaq might be tempted to come out of hiding for a whole barrel of "snacks." Then I started looking through the stack of storage boxes my folks had piled into the corner of the garage.

I was pushing aside one particularly heavy pile of junk when I heard something move over my head. Looking up, I caught a glimpse of a large toolbox that had been perched atop this pile, and before I had a chance to get out of the way, it came falling down on top of me.

When I came to, my vision was blurred, and my head felt like someone was inside it trying to blast out with dynamite. Slowly I looked around and spotted the toolbox lying open beside me, a half-dozen hand tools lying scattered on the floor nearby. There was also Shaq's barrel of snacks—overturned *and* empty.

Not knowing how long I'd been unconscious, I tried to move, but found that I couldn't.

Am I paralyzed? I wondered in panic. *Did the toolbox break my spine?*

Fortunately, my arms still worked, and I was able to lift myself into a partial sitting position. It was then that I saw why I couldn't move my legs. They were halfway down Shaq's mouth!

"Shaq, no!" I screamed, trying to kick my legs free. "Let me go, you stupid snake!"

But my movement only seemed to excite Shaq, who continued to swallow until his mouth was all the way up to my waist.

"Mom! Dad!" I yelped, pounding my fists against Shaq's big, flat snout. "Tabitha! Anybody! *HELP!*"

Then, thankfully, I heard the inner door of the garage open, and Tabitha appeared holding what looked like a big brown fuzz ball in her hands.

"Look, David, I got a new hamster!" she said with a sly smile.

"Tabitha! Get help! Shaq is trying to eat me!" I screamed as the snake's mouth worked its way up to my chest.

"Well, then, I guess that makes us even," she said calmly.

"Even?" I gasped. "Are you crazy?" I was trying to yell, but with so much pressure on my chest, I could barely choke out words, let alone scream. "Come on, Tabitha," I begged. "Help me!"

"What was that, David?" Tabitha asked. "Did you say something?"

"I'll get you for this!" I wheezed. "I swear, I'll—"

"Tabitha, find your brother!" I heard my mother call from the house. "It's time for dinner!"

Tabitha turned back to me and smiled. "It certainly is," she said. Then she looked at Shaq. "Enjoy your supper." And with that she turned and headed toward the house. "Oh, and David, say hello to my old hamster for me, will ya?" she called over her shoulder, giggling as she shut the door.

I tried to call after her, but now I could barely breathe as Shaq's mouth came all the way up to my throat. Slowly, everything was going dark, and I couldn't feel my body anymore. As I disappeared inside his cool, smooth mouth, the last thing I saw was Shaq's cold, unblinking eyes. And then I almost had to laugh as I remembered something I'd said to my snake not too long ago.

"Well, Shaq, old pal," I said, choking out the last words of my life. "I guess you took what I meant about being together forever *real* serious."

THE COLONY

Remember, dear, you have to organize your garbage every day," Julia Moritz's mother said as they stood together in the kitchen. "Aluminum cans go in the red bin, plastic bottles and containers go in the green bin, glass goes in the white bin, and all paper products go in the blue bin."

"In the end they all wind up in the same landfill anyway," Julia said with a contemptuous snort.

"That is the wrong attitude, young lady," Mrs. Moritz said sternly. "Remember, we're all part of a larger world. We have a responsibility to care for this planet, to respect nature, and to look out for all the creatures that walk the Earth."

"And that responsibility starts right here in our

own homes with recycling," Julia said mockingly. She'd heard this save-the-world speech dozens of times before. In fact, she'd heard it so many times it had lost all meaning for her. As far as Julia Moritz was concerned, the world was important only so far as it served Julia Moritz. Beyond that, she really didn't care if every endangered species kicked the bucket, if every dolphin wound up snared in a tuna net, and if the whole planet itself ended up knee-deep in garbage.

But little did Julia Mortiz know that her attitude was about to change very soon—thanks to the help of a most unexpected source.

The next morning, Julia and her best friend, Leslie Conrad, walked to school along their usual route through an empty lot overgrown with weeds and wild grasses. The lot was a favorite dumping ground for all the kids in the neighborhood, which meant that Julia and Leslie had to pick their way through a minefield of old soft drink cans, candy wrappers, abandoned toys, and other kinds of litter.

Leslie always hated having to walk through this vacant lot, but the alternate route took them a full block out of their way, so she put up with it. Julia, on the other hand, seemed to enjoy her twice-daily trip through the miniature garbage dump, so much so that she regularly contributed to its steadily growing collection of stinky junk.

On this day, for example, the girls weren't even ten feet into the lot when Julia casually tossed a toaster-pastry wrapper into the grass. A few seconds later, she nonchalantly flipped the juice box she'd just emptied to the ground as well.

Leslie stopped and put her hands on her hips. "Don't you know that's littering?"

"Hey, it's made of cardboard," Julia responded innocently. "Cardboard is made from paper, paper is made from trees, and trees are biodegradable. So what's the big deal?"

"The deal is, you're contributing to this mess," Leslie insisted, sweeping her arm across the disgusting, litter-filled lot.

"The whole world's already a mess," said Julia with a shrug. "What you or I do isn't going to make it any better or any worse, so why not just do what's easiest? I mean, life is hard enough without trying to make things *perfect*."

As Julia said this, she kicked a small anthill that rose from the ground ahead of her. Immediately, several dozen brown ants, who'd been busy collecting bits of food for their underground colony, began running around in confused disarray.

"Now why did you have to do *that*?" Leslie protested.

"Do what?" Julia asked blankly.

"Destroy their world," Leslie replied, gesturing toward the scurrying ants. "How would you like it if some giant came along and kicked *your* house over just because she felt like it?"

"But that's not going to happen," Julia pointed out with a sly smile. "We humans are at the top of the food chain. That means we can do whatever we want to, whenever we want, and there's nothing the rest of the planet can do about it. That's the natural order of things. And frankly, that suits me just fine."

As if to prove her point, Julia stepped on the remains of the anthill and ground it beneath her shoe. "See what I mean?" she said proudly. "Top of the food chain. If the ants don't like it, they can sue me."

Leslie sighed. "Julia, you know you're my best friend, but sometimes I think you are the most insensitive, irresponsible person I have ever met in my entire life,"

"Well, that's just great, Leslie," Julia said sarcastically. Then she shivered and twisted her face in disgust. "Yech! You sound just like my mother!"

When they got to school, Julia and Leslie put their differences aside and went about their usual school day routine. They got reprimanded for talking in class, switched sandwiches at lunch, and flirted with just about every cute boy they could. Everything was going along just fine until they got to their sixth-period science class. Usually Mr. Estrin, a thin, nervous man with a buzz cut, was there anxiously writing something on the board. But today Mr. Estrin was nowhere to be found. Instead, when the bell sounded to announce the start of class, a tall, dark-skinned man wearing mysterious-looking black sunglasses stepped into the room and took a position behind the teacher's desk.

"Hello, students," the man said. His voice seemed odd to Julia in a way she couldn't quite put her finger on. "My name is Mr. Anton. Your usual teacher, Mr. Estrin, can't be with you today, so I have been asked to be his substitute."

Julia and Leslie exchanged disbelieving glances. Not only had Mr. Estrin regularly boasted that he'd never missed a class in his entire fifteen years of teaching, but this new man—Mr. Anton— looked like a real weirdo. In fact, as he continued to speak, Julia realized what it was that was odd about his voice. Flat and lifeless, it sounded as if it were computerized, almost robotic. In fact, the man's movements were kind of stiff like a robot's, and he showed virtually no facial expressions.

"What's with the sunglasses?" Leslie whispered to Julia.

"I don't know," Julia whispered back. "But it sure makes him look like a geek!"

Mr. Anton snapped his head in the girls' direction. "Julia Moritz, do you have something you wish to share with the rest of the class?"

"Uh, no, sir," Julia said, sitting up in her chair, her face flushing with embarrassment. A moment later, a disturbing thought occurred to her. This Mr. Anton had entered the room just moments before. None of the students had even had a chance to introduce themselves, and he couldn't have been referring to a seating chart since the desktop was bare. So how did he know her name?

"Well, then, Ms. Moritz, if you have nothing to share, perhaps you'll keep quiet and allow me to continue," Mr. Anton said, snapping his head forward. "I understand that Mr. Estrin has just begun a section on basic biology. Although it might stray slightly from his intended course of study, I'd like to take this time to discuss one of my favorite fields of biology: the study of the insect world."

Julia sighed. As boring as Mr. Estrin's lectures were, at least his unending nervous energy always managed to keep her awake. But in just half a minute, this new teacher was already threatening to send her straight to dreamland. She'd never heard a flatter, more unemotional voice in her entire life.

"Insects, unlike so-called higher life forms, often exist as collective organisms," Mr. Anton began. "For example, the beehive and the ant colony function like single animals, with each insect member acting much like a cell in a larger body."

That's it, Julia thought. *I'm going out!*

Trying to keep herself awake, she began to doodle in her notebook. She started with abstract geometric designs, then moved quickly on to flowers and . . . insects?

Julia looked at her notebook in disbelief. She'd never doodled bugs before, but here she was sketching a bunch of bizarre-looking beetles, ants, and spiders. Like it or not, Mr. Anton's lecture was clearly having a subconscious effect on her.

"The queen of the colony functions like a brain, directing the various activities performed by the drones, workers, and soldiers," Mr. Anton continued. "The principal purpose of the colony is the same as that of any organism: survival. When attacked or disturbed, the members of a colony will act as one to protect the life of the whole, much like the biological defenses in your *human* bodies fight together to ward off an invading disease."

Julia suddenly perked up. The way Mr. Anton had emphasized the word *human* was odd. It was as though he himself wasn't, well, human . . . but that was ridiculous!

Later, as she and Leslie walked home from school through the overgrown vacant lot, Julia remarked on Mr. Anton's unusual way of speaking. "What do you suppose he meant by emphasizing the word *human* the way he did?" she asked.

"I didn't even notice it," Leslie replied, obviously unconcerned. "It's probably just the way he talks."

"And what *about* the way he talks?" Julia went

on anxiously. "He sounded like some kind of machine. I think that's maybe what he is—a robot or an android or something like that."

"I don't know much about computers, but I know they haven't made any machines that look *that* much like real people," Leslie stated. "I think maybe you're getting a little paranoid, Julia, if you ask me."

At that moment the girls arrived at the site of the anthill Julia had crushed that morning. Much to their surprise, not only had the hill been rebuilt, it was now almost twice as big as the original one.

"Well, look at that!" Leslie cried out with delight. "Nature always finds a way to fight back against bullies like you."

"Oh, yeah?" Julia scoffed. "Well, here's what I think of nature." She gave a swift kick to the new anthill, sending the fragile construction flying into a million pieces. Once again, scores of brown ants began to scurry about in a wild panic. Julia responded to their plight by crushing as many as she could under the soles of her sneakers.

"Die, you little pests!" she cried, stomping away.

Leslie shook her head in disgust. "What's wrong with you, Julia? Don't you see that they're just trying to protect their colony? It's like Mr. Anton said: They're like cells in a body. Even if you kill a hundred of them, the larger body still lives." She looked down at the dry, weed-covered ground. "In fact, if you think about it, this colony's tunnels probably go under this entire lot. That means that the ant 'body' is actually bigger than we are!"

"And look what good it does them," Julia said with a laugh. "Every anthill they build, I'm just going to knock down. And in the end, guess who's going to win?"

Leslie believed she knew the answer to that question. And it wasn't one her friend Julia was going to like.

"Julia Moritz, I'd like to see you after class," Mr. Anton said as the bell sounded the next day, announcing the end of sixth period. As the rest of the students filed out the door, Julia slowly gathered up her books, wondering what this weirdo substitute teacher could possibly want with her.

For the second day in a row, Mr. Anton had worn those odd, dark sunglasses. And for the second day in a row, he'd talked about insects, this time emphasizing their role in global ecology. In his awful monotone voice he'd droned on and on about how even the smallest of na-ture's creatures has a critical role to play in the balance of life. And he'd ended by saying that some people believe the Earth itself is nothing but one giant organism, of which all living things are an integral part.

As Julia tried to keep her eyelids from drooping, she'd thought about how her mother—the recycling queen—would love this guy. But as far as

Julia was concerned, the sooner Mr. Estrin came back, the better.

Now, as she approached Mr. Anton after class, she suddenly grew worried. Had he picked up on her hostile vibes?

Pulling herself together, she forced the friendliest smile she could onto her face, and asked Mr. Anton what she could do for him.

But to her surprise, the odd-looking substitute's face remained blank and unresponsive. Finally, after a few uncomfortable moments, he stated flatly, "We came here hoping to teach you something, Julia. We had hoped the subtle approach would be effective. Apparently we were wrong."

"I don't understand," said Julia, more confused than ever. "What do you mean, you came to teach *me*? And what do you mean by *we*?"

"Your kind may indeed be at the top of the food chain—so to speak—but that does not excuse your abusive behavior," Mr. Anton said sternly. "As a higher life form, you have a responsibility to care for both the world you inhabit and the other creatures who share it with you."

"Wait a minute, is this another ecology lecture?" Julia sighed. "Because if it is, I can get one at home any day of the week."

"Just because something is different from you doesn't mean it is *less* than you," Mr. Anton went on, ignoring what Julia had just said. "Is your heart any less valuable to you than your brain? Do you value your lungs any more than your liver? Just as organs in a body are interconnected, so are we *all* interconnected. In fact, we *all* are bound by the same great life force."

This guy has really lost it, Julia thought, growing a little afraid. But it was after what he said next that she grew terrified.

"After all," Mr. Anton continued, "how would you feel if some giant came along and kicked your house over just because she felt like it?"

Julia's jaw dropped. "That's just what Leslie asked me yesterday!"

"We know," Mr. Anton replied flatly.

"Have you been *spying* on me?" Julia asked accusingly. "Who are you? Who are you working for? What is this all about?"

His face still expressionless, Mr. Anton reached up and removed the sunglasses from his face. What Julia saw behind them made her gasp in horror.

There, in place of eyes, were two dark, fuzzy-looking pits. Looking closer, unable to believe what she was seeing, Julia saw that the fuzziness was created by movement—the movement of hundreds of tiny black objects all squirming about like maggots in a piece of rotting meat.

Although terrified beyond belief, Julia was unable to scream or run. Instead, like a moth drawn to a flame, she felt compelled to step closer. That's when she saw that Mr. Anton's "skin" wasn't really skin at all, but a surface composed of millions of tiny brown specks, much like a newspaper photo is made up of hundreds of individual dots. And, like Mr. Anton's "eyes," his "skin" also moved, as if it had a life of its own.

"We are here to tell you to leave us alone," Mr. Anton said, his voice now sounding fuzzy, as if it were coming over a distorted telephone line. "We are organized. We are strong. And we are prepared to fight back."

And then, right before Julia's disbelieving eyes, the features on Mr. Anton's face dissolved away, leaving in their place a brown, pulsating mass. His suit and pants transformed as well, until, within seconds, Julia found herself facing what looked like a human statue made of zillions of coarse grains of sand—all of which were on the move!

Ants! Julia's mind screamed. *Mr. Anton is made up entirely of ants!*

Quickly reorganizing themselves into a single, inch-wide column, the ants—acting under the orders of some distant, unseen intelligence— flowed as one across the floor and disappeared into a crack in the baseboard. A half minute later, the last of them disappeared from sight, and Julia found herself standing alone in the classroom wondering if she had, indeed, just lost her mind.

* * *

"So what did Mr. Anton have to say to you?" Leslie asked Julia as they hurried home later that afternoon.

"Nothing," Julia mumbled, her eyes glued to the pavement ahead. "I don't want to talk about it."

"Was it about your attitude?" Leslie pressed as they made their way through the trash-strewn lot.

"I said I don't—" But Julia stopped short. There, in the path ahead of her, was an anthill. The ants, industrious and determined as ever, had rebuilt their home and were back on the job of delivering food to their ant "friends" and "relatives" in the tunnels below.

This time, however, Julia didn't kick at the anthill, and she didn't try to crush any of the ants under her shoe, either. Instead, she slowly and carefully walked well around it, giving it the kind of wide berth one would give a coiled rattlesnake.

"What was *that* all about?" Leslie asked in surprise. "Are you suddenly becoming Ms. Save the World?"

"I—I—I just want to get home," Julie stammered. "I've got some garbage to sort for recycling."

Julia walked on ahead of her friend and didn't look back. If she had, she might have noticed that the ants around the hill had stopped and turned toward her. Then, as one, they formed a large dark clump, which soon turned into what looked like a knowing grin.

THE CREEPS

George Mott was the toughest kid in
Teddy Roosevelt Junior High. Nearly five and a
half feet tall and weighing close to 170 pounds, the
red-haired fourteen-year-old towered well above
most of the other kids in the eighth grade. His
arms were thickly muscular, and he had fists the
size of cantaloupes—at least they *seemed* the size
of cantaloupes to anyone George decided to beat
up. And that could be just about anybody.

Yes, George Mott was a classic bully. He'd been
big for his age for as long as he could remember,
and he enjoyed using his considerable bulk to get
his way. For example, if someone was sitting in a
chair that George wanted to sit in, he'd stand over
the silly would-be squatter and glare down at his

victim with one of his famous intimidating looks. If the poor jerk failed to get the hint in less than two seconds, George would simply pick up whoever it was and hurl him—or her—aside . . . chair and all, if he had to.

George was also well known for bullying kids out of their lunch money, pushing his way to the front of the cafeteria line, and forcing other kids to do his homework for him. Anyone who didn't comply with his wishes—and that included kids of all ages, and a few adults—risked a severe pummeling.

Those few people who did challenge George's power do to whatever he wanted to whomever he wanted usually ended up in the school nurse's office with a black eye, a bloody nose, or both. Therefore, George Mott was basically fearless. *Nothing* fazed him. He could stand on the edge of a roof three stories up, or climb a high-tension electrical tower, or scale the steep, rocky cliffs at nearby Crystal Cove confident in the knowledge that nothing in this world could ever hurt him.

In fact, in all the known universe, there was only one thing that George Mott feared. It was the one thing that set his teeth on edge, made his heart race, and caused sweat to pour down his puffy, freckle-covered cheeks. It was the sound of chalk squeaking on a blackboard.

Yes, that simple yet terribly annoying sound, which most people just shuddered at, absolutely

terrified George Mott. It made his skin crawl—
literally. For whenever he heard that awful, ultra-
high-pitched squealing, the muscles in his body
contracted in such a way that ripples of movement
would actually run up and down his arms. He
called this phenomenon "the Creeps." And, boy,
did George hate the Creeps. In fact, heaven help
anyone who caused George Mott to get them.

Since all the kids at Teddy Roosevelt Junior
High knew how much George Mott hated the
sound of squeaking chalk, they all avoided using
chalk as much as they could. If George Mott was in
your class, you never, *ever* volunteered to work a
problem out on the blackboard. And if you did
have the misfortune of being called to the board by
a teacher, you were wise to write as lightly as pos-
sible. If, heaven forbid, you did accidentally squeak
the chalk, you would leave school early and then
play sick for the next two or three days until
George's nerves had a chance to settle down.

These rules were well known to everyone at
Teddy Roosevelt Junior High—that is, to everyone
but Rudy Kazarian, an eighth grader who'd just
transferred from James Buchanan Junior High
across town. Rudy was a somewhat undersized kid
with ears that stuck out like little radar dishes. He
liked science fiction books, played the violin, and
always got A's in math. He was, in other words, the
perfect target for a bully like George Mott. And
unfortunately for Rudy, he'd been at Teddy Roo-

sevelt only forty-eight hours when he had the misfortune of unwittingly giving George Mott the Creeps.

The setting was fourth-period math class. The teacher, Mr. Lewis, had presented a complex problem and had asked if anyone would like to work the equation out on the blackboard. Of course, since George was in the class, no one raised a hand . . . no one except Rudy Kazarian.

Delighted that, for once, someone had actually volunteered to go to the blackboard, Mr. Lewis immediately called on the eager new student. Wearing a big, goony grin, Rudy walked confidently to the board, grabbed a fresh piece of chalk, and began to write.

Squeeeeeeeeaaaaakkkk!

The shrill sound cut through the air like a knife, and instantly every student in the room stopped breathing. One by one, all eyes turned toward the back of the class to where George Mott was sitting, his eyes bugging wide, his teeth clenched tight. Those students sitting next to him had the horrible opportunity to observe a phenomenon they'd never forget for the rest of their lives: George's skin actually started to *crawl*. Starting with little waves, his skin moved up and down his big, muscular arms as though worms flowed in his veins instead of blood. It was truly disgusting.

Unaware of what was going on behind him, Rudy Kazarian happily continued to work away at the problem, his back turned to the terrified class. And each time he touched the chalk to the blackboard, it let out another high-pitched *squeeeeeeaaaaaak*!

Horrified, the rest of the class watched as George Mott's jaw grew tighter, his fists grew bigger, and the ripples crawling up and down his arms moved faster with each *squeak, squeak, squeak* of the chalk.

Finally it was all over. Rudy Kazarian, certain he had solved the problem correctly, set down the chalk and turned around to face the teacher with a big, foolish grin. "Well?" he said to Mr. Lewis. "Am I right?"

"That's—uh—very good, Rudy," Mr. Lewis said nervously, for he, too, knew that the new student had just sealed his fate. "You may take your seat."

Beaming with pride, Rudy walked jauntily back to his desk. Only as he approached his seat did he realize that the class had grown completely silent, and that everyone in the room was staring at him as if some doctor had just announced that he'd contracted a dreaded disease. Rudy didn't get it. He'd written the proper equation. Mr. Lewis had praised him. What had he done wrong?

Three rows behind him, George Mott gripped the side of his desk so hard that he left actual indentations in the wood. His face was beet red, and his eyes looked ready to pop out.

Rudy Kazarian, everyone knew, was a dead man.

* * *

At three-fifteen that afternoon, George Mott's unsuspecting victim was heading for his school bus when two big kids wearing black T-shirts stepped in front of him and blocked his path.

"Excuse me," Rudy said, trying to step around them. But the two kids, Mike McLeish and Bruce Peterson, sidestepped to block his way again.

"George Mott wants to see you," Mike said with an evil smile.

"Who?" Rudy asked, oblivious to the danger he was in.

"You don't know who George Mott is?" Bruce asked, shocked.

"I'm new," Rudy confessed. "I just transferred from—"

"Well, George Mott knows who *you* are," Mike interrupted. "And he wants to see you—*now*." Without another word, Mike and Bruce each grabbed one of Rudy's arms and hauled him off.

"Hey, what are you doing?" Rudy cried in protest. "Let me go!"

Once they were safely out of sight behind a large brick wall, Mike and Bruce threw Rudy to the ground at George Mott's feet.

"You broke the rules, you little dweeb," George sneered threateningly. "Now you gotta pay the price."

"Wait!" Rudy cried, his voice quaking with fear. "What rules? What did I do?"

"You gave George the Creeps," Mike said flatly.

"The Creeps?" Rudy asked, confused. "How did I do that?"

"By squeaking chalk on the blackboard!" Bruce screamed straight into Rudy's ear. "*Everyone* knows that squeaking chalk gives George the Creeps!"

"Well, *I* didn't know!" Rudy cried, tears starting to roll down his cheeks. "Look, I promise, I'll never do it again!"

"Too late, nerd," said George, balling up his big hands, which now looked like bowling balls to poor Rudy. "I hate the Creeps. I hate people who give me the Creeps. And most of all, I hate people like *you!*"

As if on cue, Mike and Bruce lifted Rudy to his feet. A moment later, George Mott swung his arm back, then slammed his fist into Rudy Kazarian's stomach.

"I hear that Kazarian kid's going to be out of school for at least a week," Mike McLeish said to George Mott as they stood by George's locker the next day.

"Should be *two*," George grunted. "I was too easy on him. Probably because he was new."

George brutally kicked his locker shut. Then he and Mike started down the crowded hall. A few seconds later, Bruce Peterson ran up to them, panting. His face was flushed with fear.

"Hey, Bruce, what's wrong?" Mike asked. "You look like you've seen a ghost."

"I just heard something," Bruce gasped. "Something really awful."

"What?" George asked with only mild concern, for nothing fazed him. "Did that Kazarian kid call the cops or something?"

"No, he didn't call the cops," Bruce said. "He doesn't have to."

"What do you mean?" asked Mike.

"Word is, his parents are really upset," Bruce reported. "And supposedly, they're famous magicians from some weird country I can't even pronounce.

"So what?" George asked with a contemptuous laugh. "Are they going to turn me into a frog or something?"

"Worse," Bruce said. "According to some kids who know, Kazarian's parents have cast some kind of spell on you."

"Yeah, right," George scoffed. "Like I believe in magic spells. Come on, let's go grab some sodas down in the cafeteria."

George led his friends to the school lunchroom. There, along one wall, stood several vending machines. He pulled a few quarters from his pocket—quarters he'd stolen from a seventh grader earlier that morning—and popped them into the coin slot. As they slid down, George thought he heard a scraping sound, like metal on metal, and wondered if something was wrong.

"Did you hear that?" he asked Bruce.

"Hear what?" Bruce replied.

"That sound," George said, a slight shiver running up his spine. He pushed the button for a root beer, and heard an irritating, whining sound as the machine's gears turned to push the can into the vending chute. "Someone should oil this thing," George said, his face twisting in displeasure. "The noise it's making is creepy."

Bruce and Mike looked to each other in confusion. They didn't have the slightest idea what George was talking about. "Huh?" they grunted in unison.

"You don't have to scream," George exclaimed, throwing his hands over his ears. "I'm right next to you!"

George's hearing sensitivity increased throughout the day. In first-period English, while everyone wrote an essay on Nathaniel Hawthorne's *The Scarlet Letter*, George found that his pencil made such an irritating scraping sound every time he tried to put it to paper that he thought he'd scream. Not only that, he suddenly became acutely aware of similar sounds being made by *everyone's* pencils *scrape-scrape-scraping* across the paper. Unable to write anymore, George put his pencil down and covered his ears.

By third period, the mere sound of students opening and closing the spring-loaded rings on their loose-leaf binders was sending George Mott into fits of nearly uncontrollable panic. By midafternoon, the gritty sounds of girls filing their fingernails, the squeaking of athletic shoes on the school's linoleum floor, and the crunch of boys cracking their knuckles all but sent George flying through the ceiling.

"It's the spell," said Bruce as he, George, and Mike hurried away from the school after the end of their last class. "The Kazarians did this to you for beating up their kid."

George grabbed Bruce by the collar and angrily slammed him against a large oak tree.

"I told you, I don't believe in magic spells!" George bellowed. "What I did to Rudy, he deserved! The little creep was careless, and careless people get—"

But George had to stop short as his hands began quaking uncontrollably. Turning, he saw one of the boys from school riding by on his bicycle. The *clankety-clankety-clank* of the kid's bicycle chain sent a bolt of searing pain through George's head.

Gasping for air, he released Bruce and stumbled away, clamping his hands over his ears and howling in pain.

"George, what's wrong?" Mike asked in alarm.

"That sound!" George cried. "Make it stop! It's giving me the Creeps!"

As Mike and Bruce watched in silent awe, the skin on their friend's arms began to pucker and ripple. Just watching George get the Creeps was enough to make their own skin crawl, and the two boys ran away in mounting horror.

As they did, an approaching car stopped short to avoid hitting them, and the squeal of the car's tires caused George such an explosion of pain behind the eyes that he actually saw stars. A second later, somewhere in the neighborhood, a screen door squeaked closed on agonizingly rusty hinges. Two blocks away, on an athletic field, a coach blew a painfully high-pitched whistle. High in the trees, the birds sang a series of killer *tweet-tweet-tweets*. Each and every sound caused George Mott's Creeps to grow and grow until his crawling skin seemed to take on a life of its own.

"I can't stand it!" George wailed. He turned and ran headlong through the park toward Crystal Lake. A few concerned citizens gave chase after the tortured boy, but George—despite his considerable girth—was too fast for any of them.

Plunging through the park like a wild animal, his head exploding with sounds so loud and so disturbing that no human being could endure them for long without going stark, raving mad, George Mott ran and ran until he accidentally ran right off the cliffs at the edge of the park.

The cliffs, which towered above the jagged rocks of Crystal Cove thirty feet below, were surrounded by a chain-link fence. But George's case of the Creeps was so powerful that it actually propelled him right through the fence.

And as he fell toward the deadly boulders below, the last thing George Mott heard was the most terrifying sound of all: the screeching, squealing, nerve-wracking, heart-pounding, teeth-gnashing, skin-crawling sound of his own high-pitched scream.

THE OOZE MONSTER

Lana Baldridge hated high places. Being in tall buildings made her knees buckle. Driving across high bridges caused her to break out in a cold sweat. She even got light-headed riding on department store escalators. And forget about flying in airplanes!

Lana's mother and father were sensitive to their thirteen-year-old daughter's fear of heights—"acrophobia" as the doctors called it—but they didn't let it rule their lives. When necessary, they *did* go into tall buildings, drive across high bridges, and ride department store escalators. And although they had yet to fly in an airplane, they warned Laura that, sooner or later, that day would come.

"Lana, you're a teenager now. It's time to conquer your fears and go out there and explore the world," her father told her. "Remember, you can't soar like an eagle if you're afraid to take your feet off the ground."

Lana knew her father was right. She knew that her fear of heights not only was irrational but prevented her from enjoying many of life's great pleasures. And so, when her family moved from Lincoln, Nebraska, to New York City, Lana didn't protest *too* loudly when her parents decided to rent an apartment on the twenty-fifth floor of a Manhattan high-rise.

"Wow! What a view!" exclaimed Steve, her ten-year-old brother, the first time he gazed out his new bedroom window. "You can see the Empire State Building from here! And check it out! The people down there look like bugs!"

Steve motioned his big sister to the window, and reluctantly, Lana crept forward, keeping her eyes locked on the building directly across the street. She knew that if she stared straight ahead and didn't look down, she wouldn't panic . . . too much.

"This is so cool!" Steve babbled on, unable to take his eyes off the street below. "The cars look like toys. Hey, this would be a great place to drop water balloons from, wouldn't it, Lana?"

Now standing at the window, Lana held her breath and, after a minute or so, finally worked up the courage to look down at the street two hundred fifty feet below. "Y-yeah," she stammered. "P-pretty cool."

But even as her eyes ran down the length of the apartment building opposite them, Lana could feel her leg muscles grow weak and her knees begin to buckle. By the time she actually glimpsed the asphalt—which to her looked to be a million miles away—her breath was coming in short, shallow gasps and her head was swimming as if she had a high fever.

Suddenly losing her balance, Lana reached out and grabbed Steve's shoulder.

"Hey! What are you doing?" Steve shouted in alarm, for Lana had dug her fingernails into him.

"I—I have to sit down," she whispered hoarsely. She stumbled over to her brother's unmade bed and collapsed.

Steve sighed with frustration. "You know, Lana," he said, "for a teenager, you are so uncool."

Two months later, Lana had gotten used to the idea of living in a high-rise apartment . . . sort of. She still spent a lot of time in her room with her curtains drawn shut, and when she did venture out of her room and into the rest of the apartment, she always kept well away from the huge picture windows—never, *ever* getting close enough to actually see the street below.

But as terrified of heights as Lana was, she was never more scared than on the night of what became known as "the Great Storm." It was late April, a time when Old Man Winter traditionally protests summer's approach by punishing the East Coast with violent thunderstorms. On this night, the weather was particularly horrendous, so much so that, sometime around ten o'clock, Lana's building experienced a total blackout.

One minute, Lana and her brother were watching TV, and the next their world was plunged into total darkness. Nothing worked—not the lights, not the TV, not the clocks. Even the telephones were dead. And if that wasn't scary enough, outside, the wind howled and rain lashed at the windows as if some great, powerful monster was trying to break into their home and eat the Baldridge family alive.

"What happened?" Steve cried, groping around in the darkness.

"The storm must have knocked out the power," their mother said. She felt her way across the living room to the window and looked out. All the buildings around them were also pitch dark. "The whole area's blacked out. Maybe one of the transformers flooded or got hit by lightning."

"When's it going to come back on?" Lana asked fearfully.

"Who knows?" came her father's voice from somewhere in the darkness. A second later, his face was illuminated by the soft glow of the emergency candle he'd just lit. "The blackout could last a minute or it could last all night. There's no way to know with these things."

"Well, I suggest we just go straight to bed," their mother said, adding with a chuckle, "I'd say 'lights out,' but that would be kind of pointless, wouldn't it?"

Five minutes later, Lana was safely tucked into her bed. She blew out the utility candle, then pressed the "glow" dial on her wristwatch and saw that the time was 10:17. Sighing deeply, she closed her eyes and prepared to fall asleep. Outside, the storm continued to rage.

Suddenly, Lana was jolted awake by the foulest odor she had ever had the misfortune to encounter. It reeked of turpentine, rotten eggs, and her brother's sweaty gym socks. Nearly gagging, she grabbed a flashlight, slipped on her house slippers, and stumbled out into the hallway.

Steve was already in his bedroom doorway, and he shone his flashlight straight into Lana's eyes.

"Yech! What is that smell?" he groaned, making gagging noises.

"I don't know," Lana replied, completely baffled. "It smells like something died—or worse."

A moment later, Lana's mom and dad emerged from their bedroom, their flashlight beams playing on the carpet before them.

"Do you smell that?" her father asked.

"Of course we smell it!" Lana exclaimed. "You'd have to be blind not to smell it!" She thought about that last statement for a moment, then shrugged it off. It might not have made much sense, but she'd gotten her point across.

"Last week I read in the newspaper that some businesses had been accused of illegally dumping chemicals down the drains," Mrs. Baldridge said. "Solvents, paint thinner, stuff like that. Maybe the storm backed up the sewers and the chemicals somehow seeped into the building's plumbing system."

As if to confirm her mother's statement, lightning flashed and a clap of thunder shook the building to its very foundation.

"Well, I'm going to find out what's going on," Lana's father declared, going to the closet and slipping on his windbreaker. "No one can sleep with a smell like *that* in the building!"

As Lana, Steve, and their mom watched anxiously, Mr. Baldridge found the front door in the darkness and headed out into the hallway.

"I hope he'll be okay," Lana said fearfully.

"He'll be fine," her mother assured her.

But an hour later, when her father hadn't returned and the smell from the air vents had gotten worse, Lana began to feel that her father was *not* okay. In fact, she was starting to fear not just for him but for them all.

"I'm going to see what's keeping your father," Mrs. Baldridge finally said anxiously as she grabbed her house keys.

"You're going to leave us here by ourselves?" Lana asked, a chill creeping up her spine every time she glanced out at the storm still rattling the windows.

"You're in charge, Lana," her mother said, ignoring her question. "I'll be back in just a few minutes. Take care of your brother. And don't let any strangers in while I'm gone."

She gave each of her children a light kiss on the cheek, then disappeared into the dark hallway.

"This really stinks," Lana said with a sigh, shutting and locking the front door.

"You're not kidding," Steve said, pinching his nose. "Peeee-youuu!"

"I mean this storm," Lana said, collapsing into one of the living room chairs. "And the black-out. And being stuck twenty-five stories up in the air!"

"*And* not being able to watch TV!" Steve added with a pout.

For nearly an hour, Lana sat in the darkness, trying to ignore the nauseating smell. Steve was glued to the window, watching the storm, barely saying a word except for an occasional "Wow!" as lightning lanced down from the sky.

With the smell growing worse by the second, Lana was going nuts. Finally, when her digital watch read exactly half past midnight, she could stand it no more. She got to her feet, grabbed her robe and flashlight, and headed for the front door.

"Where are you doing?" asked Steve, turning away from the window.

"To find Mom and Dad," Lana replied as she tripped open the dead bolt. "They shouldn't have been gone this long."

"What about *me*?" Steve whined, showing genuine fear for the first time the entire evening. "You're not going to leave me here by myself, are you?"

"I'll be back in ten minutes, I promise," said Lana. "In the meantime, keep the door locked."

Lana stepped out of the apartment and shone her flashlight down the hallway. Out here, the awful smell was even stronger than it had been inside, and it caused her eyes to tear.

Creeping down the hall, she stopped in front of the elevators and pushed the "down" button. But it didn't light up. She pushed it again, and when it still failed to light, Lana realized that, of course, with the power out, the elevators wouldn't be working. That meant if she was going to get down to ground level, she'd have to take the stairs—all twenty-five flights.

"This *really* stinks," Lana grumbled to herself, then turned and walked over to the emergency stairway.

The door, which had been designed to resist fires, was quite heavy, and it took an extra effort for Lana to push it open. When she did, she was hit square in the face with a stench far worse than the one she'd been enduring all evening.

Taking a few seconds to steel herself against the horrific odor, Lana slowly walked onto the landing and shone her flashlight down the stairs.

She couldn't believe what she saw.

There, on the landing a half flight below, was some kind of thick, green slime covered with tiny red pimples. Undulating like a giant amoeba, the slime was working its way up the stairs. Worse, the repulsive stuff she could see appeared to be only a small section of its main body. The rest of the slime ran down the stairs, disappearing into darkness.

Worst of all, something was sticking out from the slime. At first it appeared to be a hairy growth of some kind, but when Lana shone her flashlight on it, she saw that it was a head—the head of a stray cat she'd seen roaming around the building. Too terrified to scream, Lana gagged as the cat's head was sucked into the slime, disappearing forever.

That did it. Lana instantly found the voice to scream. And scream she did. It echoed up and down the metal stairwell, amplifying with each terror-filled reverberation.

Seemingly attracted to the sound, the foul-smelling ooze increased its speed as it continued to crawl up the staircase. Realizing that the awful thing would be upon her in seconds, Lana spun on her heels, threw open the fire door as if it weighed nothing, and raced back into the hallway.

"Open the door!" she cried as she pounded her fists on the locked apartment door.

"Who is it?" Steve asked from the other side in a teasing, singsongy voice.

"Open up, you idiot!" screamed Lana as she heard the shattering of glass behind her. She whipped around, directing the flashlight beam down the hall. The monstrous ooze had used the pressure of its enormous body to push out the fire door's small inset window. Now it was pouring itself through the opening and collecting in a pool on the hallway floor.

As Lana watched in horror, another apartment door opened down the hall and Mrs. Williams, a sweet old lady who'd lived in the building for probably a hundred years, stepped out to see what all the commotion was about. The next instant, the ooze launched itself at her like a snake snaring a field mouse. It wrapped a slimy tentacle around the old woman's ankles and quickly drew her toward its body, as if preparing to gobble down a snack.

"Help!" Mrs. Williams screamed, seeing Lana down the hall. "It's got me!"

Bravely running to the poor woman's aid, Laura stopped when she saw that the ooze had already sucked Mrs. Williams into its core. Realizing that nothing could be done for her unfortunate neighbor, Lana turned and ran back to her apartment. "Let me in, Steve, or I'll kill you!" she screeched, flinging herself at the door.

Obviously sensing that Lana's terror was genuine, Steve threw back the dead bolt, and Lana burst inside, slamming the door firmly behind her.

"What is it?" Steve asked, his eyes wide with fear.

"I—I don't know," Lana stammered. "Some kind of monstrous ooze probably created by those chemicals Mom was talking about. Whatever it is, it's alive, it's gigantic, and it's eating everyone in the building!"

Steve gulped. "Do you think it ate Mom and Dad?"

"I don't know," Lana replied. "Maybe they got out of the building somehow. That's what we're going to have to do. But first we have to keep that thing from getting in here!"

With that, Lana quickly double-locked the door, then rushed to the hallway linen closet, where she grabbed several towels. Returning to the living room, she forced the towels into the thin crack at the bottom of the door, hoping that would slow the slime creature's advance for at least a few precious moments.

"Lana, look!" Steve shouted as Lana was putting the last towel in place. He was shining his flashlight at one of the living room air vents. Green, red-speckled slime was pouring from the vent into the apartment. With it came an odor that nearly knocked Lana out cold.

"Come on!" she shouted, grabbing her brother's hand. "Maybe the bedrooms are safe!"

Lana stumbled through the darkness toward her bedroom. In the confusion she slammed her leg into an end table, losing her grip on the flashlight and Steve's hand in the process.

"Steve!" she cried, reaching back, trying to find him.

"Lana, help!" came her brother's voice from the darkness. "It's got me!"

Locating the flashlight on the floor. Lana snapped on the beam and shone it back toward the living room. There, just five feet behind her, Steve was flailing his arms wildly as a tentacle of green, pockmarked ooze drew him into the monster's body.

"No!" Lana screamed, trying to grab her brother's hand. But as she did, another tentacle lashed out to grab her. It missed her arm by mere inches, but in the process the slime managed to swallow her brother whole.

With Steve's terrified face forever imprinted in her mind, Lana turned and sprinted the remaining fifteen feet to her bedroom. There she slammed the door and looked around frantically for a weapon.

It's hopeless, she thought. *It's going to get me and there's nothing I can do. There's no way out!*

A brilliant lightning flash drew Lana's attention to her bedroom window. She raced over to it, drew back the curtains, and searched desperately for a lock or a handle. But, as in most modern high-rise buildings, these windows couldn't be opened. The building was designed to be artificially air-conditioned, not heated and cooled by the outside air.

Spinning around, Lana saw a finger of green ooze sliding through the crack beneath her door. The monster would be upon her in seconds.

I'm not going to let it take me, Lana thought. *I won't go that way. I'd rather die first.*

Her heart pounding wildly, Lana grabbed the chair beside her desk and hurled it at the window. There was a deafening crash as the glass shattered into thousands of shards that fell away into the stormy night.

Momentarily forgetting her acrophobia, Lana stepped up onto her desk and looked out through the open window. Rain was still falling in sheets. She looked out farther and could see traffic trying to move in the darkness.

With sweat pouring down her face, Lana considered what she was about to do. Her legs grew weak and her hands shook uncontrollably. Her stomach was already in knots from the mere sight of the street from this height. But what choice did she have?

Crying, she looked back and saw that the slime thing had pressed its way into her room and was now almost upon her. In just a few more moments, she would suffer the same awful fate as her brother, and probably her parents.

Nothing could be worse than that, Lana thought, imagining herself being digested alive inside this awful slime beast. *Nothing!*

Taking a deep breath, she turned to the open window and prepared to jump.

But just at that moment, a huge gust of wind roared past the building, sending a powerful spray of rainwater through the window. Already drenched from head to toe, Lana saw that the slime creature had been soaked as well. And as it got wet, it slid backwards, retreating from the continuing spray.

That's it! Lana's mind screamed. *The monster hates water!*

For a few more seconds, Lana remained in the window, holding her ground while the monster behind her continued to move back and forth, trying to find a way to grab her without getting itself wet. Unwilling to settle for this uncomfortable standoff, Lana racked her brain for some other way to douse the monster with water. . . . Then she saw the emergency fire sprinkler attached to the ceiling.

Wondering if the system would work even during this blackout, Lana kept one eye on the frustrated slime monster as she slowly bent down and picked up the utility candle she'd left on the desktop earlier that evening. A book of matches lay beside it.

Her hands shaking, Lana awkwardly held the candle and somehow managed to strike a match. Shielding the tiny flame from the wind with her body, she lifted the burning candle up towards the fire sprinkler and held it there with her trembling hand.

Several excruciatingly long seconds ticked by until, finally, the ceiling above her practically exploded with water. Clearly operating by an emergency power source, the fire sprinkler sensed the heat of the candle and responded in the way it had been programmed.

"Hooray!" Lana cried as glorious man-made rain, cold and hard, poured into her room. Then, laughing with hysterical glee, she watched as the slime monster thrashed its tentacles about wildly, reacting to the water the same way people would react to sulfuric acid. Steam rose from its wildly undulating body as the mutated ooze dissolved away.

The bedroom doorway suddenly clear, Lana rushed out into the hallway and saw that water was pouring from all the apartment's overhead sprinklers. As it did, the creature's enormous body—which stretched all the way back into the living room air vents—dissolved into nothing but a thin, gooey film.

Laughing and crying at the same time, Lana slid down the wall she'd been leaning against and sat on the soaking wet carpet while water continued to pour down from overhead. She thought about her brother and how she'd nearly shared his gruesome fate. And she made a silent wish that somehow her parents had survived. She wanted them to know how brave and clever she'd been, how she'd conquered her fear of heights and had even been prepared to jump a full twenty-five stories if that's what it took to get away from the slime.

She wondered if she'd ever have that chance.

Fifteen minutes later, responding to a distress signal from the battery-powered computer in Lana's apartment building, a unit of three fire trucks arrived to handle the emergency. The elevators were still not operating, and apparently some horrible acid spill had eaten away whole sections of the building's stairway.

The people who had survived the ooze attack had to be evacuated. For Lana Baldridge, this was no problem. While a team of firefighters waited below around a huge, inflated air bag, Lana stood in her shattered window, then calmly launched herself into space.

Her parents, who *were* among the survivors, watched in amazement from below as their daughter sailed through the air. They waited for Steven. And waited.

Much later, after the grief over her brother's death had eased, Lana would realize that among the many deaths that evening had been the "death" of her acrophobia. It was one monster that would haunt her no more.

THE FIVE DIGITS OF DEATH

The car ride from Ithaca, New York, to San Diego, California, was supposed to take five days. Sam Latimer's father, however, insisted they could actually do it in three, but Sam's mom didn't want to spend more than eight hours a day on the road. So after a short debate, everyone agreed that a five-day schedule would be far more comfortable for everybody.

Well, not *everybody*. Sam had wanted to do the trip in just *one* day. He had wanted to fly. But since the family was moving across the country, and had to move their car along with everything else, driving seemed the logical way to go.

It was a decision everyone would long regret.

Day three of the Latimers' coast-to-coast drive

found the family deep in the heart of central
Texas. Mr. and Mrs. Latimer were in the front seat
listening to country western music—it seemed to
be the only kind of music the radio could pick up—
while Sam played a hand-held video game. He and
his younger brother, Felix, were supposed to share
the game, but Sam, being thirteen and older, kept
it mostly to himself.

Meanwhile, Felix, who was nine, grew bored and
started playing with the power window button.
He'd lower the window a bit, raise it back, lower it
a little farther, then raise it back, driving everyone
crazy.

Mr. Latimer quickly grew annoyed with his
younger son's antics. "Stop playing with your
window!" he snapped. "It's not a toy!"

Felix jerked back in his seat, the picture of innocence. "I wasn't doing anything," he said, wide-
eyed. "Gosh, a guy can't even get a little air!"

"Don't lie," said Sam. "You were too playing
with the window."

"Was not!" Felix said in his best bratty voice.

"Were, too!" Sam shot back.

"That's enough!" their mother said firmly. "Just
sit back and behave, the both of you! We still have
a long trip ahead of us, and I don't want to spend it
listening to you two fight!"

Sam turned and gave Felix a smug, superior
smile. Felix sneered back at him. He'd always
resented Sam's arrogant attitude. But he knew that

someday their four-year age difference wouldn't mean anything. Yes, Felix knew that someday Sam wouldn't have the upper hand, and he sure looked forward to that day. Then he'd show his big brother who was boss.

Another hour passed, and the landscape remained unendingly flat, brown, and virtually featureless. Once again, Felix grew restless.

With Sam still distracted by his video game, Felix returned to toying with the power window button. He first ran his index finger over its smooth plastic surface. Then he applied a little pressure to the "down" arrow. With a hum, the window lowered an inch. He quickly pressed the "up" arrow, and it snapped closed with a motorized thump.

Felix looked around nervously. Sam was looking at him out of the corner of his eye, but hadn't said anything yet. In fact, Sam was hoping that Felix would continue to play with the window. He enjoyed nothing more than seeing his kid brother get into trouble.

Believing that no one was watching him, Felix now lowered the window all the way, letting the hot, humid Texas air blast into his face at seventy miles per hour.

"Dad, Felix is playing with the window again!" Sam finally cried above the roar of the wind. He didn't care about being a tattletale as long as it ruined Felix's fun.

"Hey, look!" Felix pointed to a herd of cows grazing in a field at least a quarter-mile away. He stuck his hand out the window and waved. "Race you to San Diego, you stupid cows!" he yelled.

"I said stop playing with the window!" Mr. Latimer snapped again. He angrily pushed the "up" switch on his master control panel. Immediately, Felix's window began to rise . . . with his hand still outside.

Sam saw what was happening, but said nothing.

As Felix tried to yank his hand back into the car, his wrist got caught by the ascending glass. His hand was cut off cleanly at the wrist!

Mrs. Latimer, screaming in horror, shouted at her husband to stop the car. Mr. Latimer, who still didn't know what he'd done, slammed on the brakes and pulled off to the side of the road.

Seeing all the blood, Mr. Latimer threw the car keys at Sam and told him to get the towels they kept in the trunk. "We—we'll need to wrap that wound," he stammered, his face now as white as his wife's. "Then Felix will stay here in the car while we look for his hand."

Sam, too shocked to do anything but nod his head robotically, climbed out of the car and walked back to the trunk. He couldn't believe what had just happened. And he couldn't believe Felix's reaction—he didn't even seem to *have* one.

In fact, Felix hadn't said a word. Not a tear. Not a whimper. Nothing. He didn't seem to be in any pain, either. Later, a doctor said that Felix was suffering from shock, that his brain, realizing what had happened, had just shut down. He just sat in the back seat holding a bloody towel around his right wrist while the rest of the family scrambled around the shoulder of the highway searching for the severed hand.

"We've *got* to find it!" Mrs. Latimer insisted hysterically as she paced through the wispy strands of dried sagebrush. "It can be reattached. But we've got to find it!"

Mr. Latimer nodded weakly. "Your mother's right," he called to Sam, who was about ten feet away following a trail of blood drops. "Keep looking!"

But they couldn't find Felix's right hand anywhere. It was as if the thing had just crawled away on its own to . . . well, die.

Finally, Mr. Latimer said it was time to get Felix to a hospital, "hand or no hand." Fortunately, there was a medium-sized town only ten miles up the interstate, and the emergency room doctors were able to properly treat Felix's injury.

Because of the tragic accident, the Latimers arrived at their new home in San Diego a week behind schedule, and the ride from central Texas to southern California was, needless to say, unusually quiet. Everyone was afraid to say anything that might start an argument about who was responsible for the loss of Felix's hand, so the best alternative seemed to be a deathly silence.

Sam felt particularly guilty. He had seen Felix start to play with the window, but had said nothing. Then, when his father had shut the window from the front seat, he hadn't shouted for Felix to pull in his hand. He believed that he, and he alone was responsible for his kid brother's injury. And although Felix never said a word about it, Sam was sure that his brother felt the same way.

The first night in San Diego proved to be a very difficult one for Sam. Alone in the dark, he kept replaying the accident over and over in his mind. Then he began to think about his brother lying in the next bedroom. Without his right hand, Felix would never do so many of the things other kids got to. He'd never play baseball. He'd have a hard time operating a computer keyboard. And because he was right-handed, not only he would have to learn to write with his left hand, but he'd also have to figure out how to do everything else backwards. Felix's whole life was bound to change, to become more difficult . . . all because of Sam.

After that first guilt-ridden night, each night afterward was a nightmare for Sam. As he lay in bed trying to shake off his dark thoughts, he only succeeded in growing more and more restless. Finally, on his eighth night in their new home, Sam fell into a deep sleep, only to be awakened by an odd noise coming from somewhere in the house. It was a dull, scraping sound, like something being dragged along a hard surface.

At first, Sam tried to ignore the noise—new homes were always filled with odd bumps, creaks, and thumps—but this sound was persistent. Finally it started to freak Sam out.

His heart beating rapidly, his throat dry, Sam strained his ears and turned his head from side to side trying to locate where the sound was coming from. Then he heard a distant metallic clang and realized that something was moving around inside the air ducts.

For the next hour he sat up in bed listening to whatever was making the noise skitter about in the ducts that linked the various rooms of their single-story home. Finally, around four in the morning, all was quiet, and Sam was able to drift back into a shallow, fitful sleep.

The next morning, he told his parents about the bizarre noise. His father took the news with surprising calmness.

"Probably some animal got into the ducts through the air-conditioning system," he said around a mouthful of cold cereal and milk. "I'll have an exterminator come in and take a look."

But the Pest-B-Gone man who showed up that afternoon could find no sign of any animal. In fact, as far as he could see, the duct system was completely sealed. There was no way an animal could get in or out of the ducts, unless it had fingers to open and close the access panel on the outside air-conditioning unit. "Maybe it was the wind," the exterminator suggested, then added with a laugh, "or a ghost!"

Somewhat relieved, Sam went to bed that night, safe in the knowledge that no creepy little animals were running to and fro in the air ducts. However, at around two in the morning, he was again awakened by the unmistakable sound of movement coming from behind the air vent . . . the one mounted right above his bedroom door.

Working up the courage to investigate, Sam quietly slipped out of bed and grabbed the flashlight he always kept in his desk's upper drawer. The scraping sounds continued to echo from the vent as he carefully approached it. Finally, when he was standing directly underneath it, he held his breath and directed the flashlight beam toward the vent. What he saw made his eyes practically pop out of his head.

There, just behind the vent's grating, was a human hand.

At first, Sam's mind tried to make sense of it by imagining that a small man had somehow gotten into the ducts and was trying to remove the vent to his bedroom. But when the hand, which was clearly startled by the light, turned around and *ran away*, Sam could see that no body was attached to it.

That was enough to unleash a scream from Sam like none other he'd ever screamed before. In seconds, his mother and father came dashing into his bedroom, still dazed from sleep.

"What's wrong?" they cried in unison.

"B-b-behind the vent," Sam managed to stammer out. "I saw a hand!"

"A *what*?" his mother asked, confused.

"A hand!" Sam shouted. Then, in a flash, he understood what was happening. "It was Felix's hand. It must have followed us all the way from Texas! It's come to get me!"

"You're saying Felix's hand is *alive*?" His father struggled to stifle a laugh. "Even if it was, how would it get here? Hitchhike?"

For a moment, Sam imagined Felix's disembodied hand standing on a Texas highway, its thumb stuck out for a ride. Of course, the whole thing seemed ridiculous. Even so . . .

"I know what I saw!" Sam insisted. "There was a hand in the air duct. And I think it was Felix's!"

"Well, I think you just had a bad dream," his mother said. Then she took the flashlight from her son's trembling fingers and directed him back into his bed. "Go back to sleep and everything will be fine in the morning."

"I know what I saw," Sam said weakly after his mother had tucked him in like she used to when he was a little kid. "It was Felix's hand, and it's come to get me."

Oddly enough, Felix slept through the whole thing.

The next three days passed without any reappearance of the hand that had supposedly crawled all the way from Texas to California. Naturally, Sam told Felix what he had seen, but his kid brother seemed strangely unconcerned that his missing hand might now be crawling around the house. In fact, Felix seemed to enjoy the idea. Sam had always been the "mature" one, the "strong" one, and Felix liked seeing his older brother be the one who was weak and acting like a baby.

"Maybe now you'll treat me a little better," Felix said with a sly smile. "Maybe now you won't grab the best pieces of fried chicken, or hog the remote control, or take my video-game cartridges without asking."

"Maybe you'll just shut up and stay in your place," Sam replied, no longer feeling quite so sorry for his injured brother. "I don't care if you did lose your hand. I'm still the older brother, and I'm still the one who deserves to be in charge."

"Oh, yeah?" Felix said. "We'll see about that."

Sam went to bed that night unsure what sick, twisted schemes Felix had in mind. But he found out soon enough when, just after drifting off to

sleep, he was awakened by the feeling of someone—
or some*thing*—clutching his throat.

"What the—?" he managed to blurt out, only to
be cut short when a viselike grip choked off his
words. Flailing wildly, Sam tried to push away
whoever was trying to strangle him—but there
was no one there.

Reaching for his neck, he was stunned to dis-
cover that, yes, there was a hand around his
throat. But that's all there was—just a hand, no
arms, no body. It was his brother's hand—Sam
was sure of that now—and somehow it had taken
on a life of its own.

"Help! Help!" Sam choked out, trying to pull the
horrific hand away. It was remarkably strong for
having once belonged to a nine-year-old, and it was
terribly cold—*ice* cold—like the hand of Death
itself.

His lungs now aching as they struggled for air,
Sam felt himself growing weak. A few more
moments of this agony, and he was certain he
would die.

And then a voice called out from the darkness. It
was Felix.

"Stop!" his brother commanded. "Let him go!"

Amazingly, the pressure on Sam's throat suddenly relaxed, and he made a sick, wheezing sound
as he sucked in lungfuls of air.

"Come," Felix ordered, speaking to his hand.
"That's enough for now."

His eyes wide, Sam watched in horrified amazement as the hand released his throat and jumped down onto his bed. Then, using its fingertips like five little legs, it skittered over the covers, leaped into the air, and landed in an open shoe box Felix was holding in the crook of his right arm.

"Neat, huh?" Felix said, calmly putting the lid on the box with his left hand. "I found my hand two days ago . . . or rather, it found *me*. Anyway, it does whatever I say."

"W-w-what are you going to do with it?" Sam asked in a trembling voice.

"Keep it, of course," Felix said. "It *is* mine, after all, isn't it?"

He turned as if to go, then looked back at his older brother.

"Don't tell Mom and Dad about this. Don't tell *anyone* . . . or my hand might get angry," he warned. "Oh, and by the way, the next time Mom makes fried chicken, you'd better let *me* take the best pieces. And from now on, *I'll* decide what we watch on TV, okay? And one more thing, I'd better not *ever* see you lay a finger on my video games, understand?"

Sam nodded weakly, and was speechless as he watched his brother disappear into the dark hallway, his shoe box tucked confidently under his arm. "If I think of anything else I want," Felix whispered from the shadows, "I'll let you know."

Trembling from head to toe, Sam fell back onto his pillow and heaved a painful sigh. As much as he hated to admit it, things had definitely changed. Yes, it looked like from now on, when it came to their relationship, Felix would definitely have the upper hand.

DON'T LET THE
BEDBUGS BITE

Good night! Sleep tight! Don't let the bedbugs bite!"

Lisa Carpenter's mother had recited this classic bedtime rhyme to her every night for the past thirteen years. Even though Lisa was now in the eighth grade, she never went to bed without hearing her mother say it. In fact, even if her mother was out of town on business, she never failed to call and recite the little rhyme over the phone.

It was a ritual that Lisa had never questioned, and Lisa had come to feel it was like saying, "God bless you" when someone sneezed, or "Fine" when someone asked how you were. It was just something that came out of a person's mouth at a given time. It was just something that, well, *always* happened.

But all that changed the night Lisa's best friend, Jennifer, slept over. It was ten-thirty on a Saturday night, and the two had just settled into their sleeping bags after a long evening of videos, snacks, and talking about boys.

"Good night! Sleep tight! Don't let the bedbugs bite!" Lisa's mother called from the living room.

"Night, Mom!" Lisa called in return.

"What was *that* all about?" Jennifer asked in a low voice.

"What do you mean?" asked Lisa. "What was *what* all about?"

"That 'Don't let the bedbugs bite' thing," Jennifer replied. "It's kind of babyish, don't you think?"

"Not really," Lisa said defensively. "I mean, it's just a little rhyme. It's something my mom says to me every night. You know, like a tradition."

A few moments passed in uncomfortable silence. Then Jennifer asked, "What *are* bedbugs, anyway?"

At first, Lisa wasn't sure how to respond. Until now, she hadn't really given the matter much thought.

"To tell you the truth, I don't even know if there *are* such things," she said with a shrug.

"They sound pretty creepy," Jennifer said with a shiver. "Maybe they're like the fleas my dog brings into the bed when she sleeps with me.

Sometimes I'll wake up and my arm will be covered with fleabites—especially in the summer. Boy, do they itch!"

"I don't think they're fleas," Lisa offered with a grin. "Then everyone would say, 'Good night. Sleep tight. Don't let the *fleas* bite.' "

Jennifer rolled her eyes. "Then maybe they're like cockroaches," she suggested, trying to get to the bottom of this bedbug issue. "A friend of mine used to live in Miami, and she said they had these awful flying cockroaches there. The people call them palmetto bugs. One night she got into bed and felt something bite her big toe. When she threw back the covers, she found a cockroach the size of her dad's *thumb*."

"Eeewww!" Lisa squealed, instinctively kicking her feet around the bottom of her sleeping bag as if to seek out any palmetto bugs that might have made the two-thousand-mile trip from Miami to her house in Las Cruces, New Mexico.

"Or maybe bedbugs are those microscopic horned insects that live in people's mattresses," Jennifer went on relentlessly.

Lisa shuddered. "What are you talking about?"

"It was something I saw on TV," Jennifer explained. "These tiny insects that look like itty-bitty rhinoceroses. They live in mattresses."

"Everyone's?" Lisa exclaimed in disbelief.

"Everyone's," Jennifer said confidently. "Even

rich people's. There are millions of them in your mattress, and there's nothing you can do about them."

"Do they bite?" asked Lisa, her eyes wide.

"Probably," Jennifer said.

"Maybe they *are* the bedbugs in the rhyme," Lisa said, pulling the sleeping bag tightly around her. She imagined her mattress infested with tiny rhinoceros-like insects, and was glad she wasn't sleeping in her bed tonight. In fact, after what her friend Jennifer had just said, she wondered if she'd be able to sleep on her mattress—or *any* mattress—ever again.

The next morning, the mystery of the bedbugs continued to plague Lisa. Equally curious about what these insects might be, Jennifer suggested that they look the subject up in the CD-ROM encyclopedia Lisa had gotten for her thirteenth birthday.

"Good idea," Lisa said, and right after breakfast, that's exactly what they did.

Having worked with computers since she was eight, Lisa had no problem booting up the system her family had set up in the basement. She slid the silvery CD-ROM disc into the receptor slot, waited a few moments while the machine whirred to life, then smiled as the encyclopedia's colorful logo appeared on the monitor screen.

"How should I start the search?" Lisa asked her friend. "With the word *insects* or *mattresses*?"

"I'd go straight for the word *bedbugs*."

Lisa quickly typed B-E-D-B-U-G-S in the appropriate window, then clicked on the return key. Again, the CD-ROM disc drive whirred for a few seconds. Then a list of references appeared on the screen. Using the mouse, Lisa pointed the cursor arrow and clicked on what looked like the most interesting article: *"Bedbugs bugging you?"*

Instantly, a short article appeared on the screen. It read: *Bedbugs are small, flat-bodied insects that infest homes and bedding. Their scientific name is Cimex lectularius. Found worldwide, these wingless, odorless insects measure about a quarter-inch long and are parasites that feed on blood.*

Lisa's face twisted in disgust. "Blood!" she groaned. "I have parasites living in my bed and they're feeding on my blood!"

"I wouldn't worry about it," Jennifer said nonchalantly. "It's not like you're going to die from having a little bit of blood drained out of your body while you sleep. I mean, that hasn't happened to anyone yet or it would've been all over the news."

But Lisa *did* worry about it. In fact, over the next several days, the idea of bedbugs soon became an obsession. All she could think about was having thousands of tiny insects popping out of her sheets while she slept, crawling up her arms, legs, and torso, and then proceeding to suck the living blood from her veins.

It wasn't a fate she was going to accept easily.

"I want to wash my sheets," Lisa told her mother after two days of sleeping on the floor.

"But I just washed them three days ago," her mother replied. "Did you spill something on them? You know I don't like you eating in bed."

"I wasn't eating in bed," Lisa replied. "I—I just feel like my sheets are dirty. In fact, I want to wash them every day . . . and my pajamas, too."

"Lisa, what's wrong?" Mrs. Carpenter asked, concerned about her daughter's sudden odd behavior. "You never seemed interested in how often I did the laundry before."

"I don't want to get bedbugs," Lisa said matter-of-factly. "Maybe if we had clean sheets and pajamas every night—"

"*Bedbugs?*" her mother said in surprise. "What are you talking about?"

Lisa explained that, after years of hearing "Good night. Sleep tight. Don't let the bedbugs bite," she'd finally learned that bedbugs were actually horrible little bloodsucking creatures that got into people's bedding if they weren't careful.

"You're being ridiculous," her mother insisted. "We don't have bedbugs. I don't know anybody who *does* have bedbugs."

"Then why do you say that rhyme every night before I go to bed?" Lisa demanded.

"It's just something I remember from when *I* was a little girl," her mother explained. "It probably goes back a hundred years to when bedbugs *were* a real problem. But they're not anymore, honey, believe me."

"Even so, I just want to be safe," Lisa insisted.

"Suit yourself," Mrs. Carpenter replied with a shrug. "In fact, you're welcome to wash *all* our sheets as often as you'd like."

But even sleeping in freshly washed pajamas on freshly washed sheets, Lisa couldn't get comfortable.

They're in the mattress, she thought, staring into the darkness of her bedroom. *Thousands of them are just waiting for me to fall asleep so they can suck my blood.*

Afraid to close her eyes, Lisa just lay there, her heart fluttering over every creak, moan, click, and thump she heard throughout the night. Finally, around three-thirty in the morning, exhaustion caught up with her and she drifted off into a restless sleep filled with nightmares about tiny, vampirelike rhinoceros bugs.

Consequently, the next day at school she was exhausted and could barely pay attention in class. Her eyes felt as if they were made of lead, and they threatened to shut even when she pinched herself.

Jennifer noticed that Lisa wasn't her usual lively self and asked her what was wrong during lunch.

"I couldn't sleep last night," Lisa explained wearily. "All I could think about were those stupid bedbugs. I'm afraid they're going to kill me in the middle of the night."

"Right, like that happens all the time," Jennifer said sarcastically. "Every day, the newspapers are filled with stories about armies of bloodsucking bedbugs killing kids in their sleep. It's an epidemic!"

"I know it's silly, but I can't stop thinking about it," Lisa insisted. "The bugs are real, especially if they're in the encyclopedia. Maybe they're more of a problem than people recognize."

"Get some sleep, Lisa," Jennifer said, putting a friendly arm around her friend's shoulder. "Things will look much better when your brain's working right."

But that night, Lisa awoke with a start around two o'clock. There was a painful itching sensation on her right leg. Bolting up in her bed, she threw back the covers, snapped on the bedside lamp, and tried to focus her sleepy eyes on the area above her right knee.

Sure enough, there was a tiny red spot just above her kneecap. It was about the size of a pea. Now, at any other time, Lisa would have concluded that she'd been bitten by a mosquito or something equally harmless, but tonight there was only one cause that came to her tortured mind.

"Bedbugs!" she gasped.

Choking back a scream, Lisa leaped out of bed and stripped the covers off her mattress. Although she expected to find the bed crawling with tiny, red, flat-bodied insects, she found only the familiar quilting of her mattress cover.

She then threw the sheets back onto the bed and flattened them out, sure she would find some evidence of the infestation she feared. But the sheets looked as clean and white as they had when she'd gone to bed four hours earlier.

Still too upset to go back to sleep, Lisa lay on the unmade bed until the sun rose in the eastern sky. Then, feeling so tired it felt like she was moving through molasses, she weakly got herself dressed, forced down a light breakfast, and trudged the four and a half blocks to school.

It took all the energy Lisa could muster just to get herself through the school day. Walking through the crowded halls like a zombie, she kept bumping into people, often forgetting where she was headed. She spent half the time in class with her head on her desk and, several times, failed to respond when she was called on by her teachers.

Finally, when the last bell rang, she stumbled gratefully from the building and started home, eager to lie down on her living room couch and sleep for the next fifty years.

But Lisa got only as far as Humbolt Park, a small recreation area two blocks from her home, before her exhaustion finally caught up with her. Feeling weak and light-headed, she walked over to a large shade tree, set down her books, then sat back against the tree trunk.

I'll just rest for a while, she told herself. *I'll be fine after a little nap.*

Certain she was safe from any of the blood-sucking creatures, Lisa allowed herself to close her eyes and, seconds later, she was fast asleep.

When Lisa awoke several hours later, she was surprised to see that the sun had already set in the western sky. And since night falls quickly in the New Mexican desert, the air—which had been warmer than usual—was already noticeably cool.

"I've got to get home!" Lisa cried. "Mom and Dad must be worried sick about me!"

Shaking her head to clear it, she realized what a fool she'd been. How could she have been afraid of bedbugs? She'd lived thirteen full years without ever having seen one. None of her friends ever complained about them. Heck, they probably didn't even exist in places like New Mexico.

I'm going to be fine, she thought happily. *Nothing's going to suck my blood in the middle of the night. In fact, I'm going to forget about bedbugs for the rest of my life.*

But as she tried to get up, Lisa felt as if her arms had suddenly burst into flames. Alarmed, she looked down and saw that both arms were covered with swollen, red-ringed welts. While she had slept, dozens of mosquitoes had bitten her, pumping their awful toxins into her veins as they fed on her blood.

Then Lisa felt hot flaming pain roar up her legs. Fire ants—millions of them!—covered her feet and calves like a blanket of bubbling molasses. Pouring from anthills all around her, the horrible creatures were moving quickly up her body, gnawing her exposed flesh.

Screaming, Lisa jumped to her feet and beat at the ants. At the same time clouds of mosquitos swarmed all about her face as she blinked to keep them from biting her eyes. Her nose and mouth were thick with bugs. It was no use. The more she tried to fight, the worse it seemed. *She was being eaten alive!*

It couldn't get much worse. Then, she looked up into the tree above her. Dozens of yellow eyes were staring back at her.

Lisa recognized them immediately. Vampire bats. Awakened from their slumber by the fragrant aroma of blood—*her* blood!

Lisa started to laugh. *This is amazing!* she thought, driven to laughter at the incredible irony of her predicament. Her childish fear of bedbugs had driven her to the safety of outdoors—where, improbably, she was being eaten alive.

Her laughter rose and rose until it turned into a shrill, hysterical scream. For it was at that moment that, as one, the vampire bats descended in a great, fluttering cloud for their bloody feast.

TOR BOOKS

Itching for something really scary?

Quit buggin' and check out these other titles in the Crawlers series. The stories are so scary they'll have you crawling back for more!

□ **The Roaches' Revenge & Other Creepy Tales**
0-812-54357-2 $4.99/$6.50 CAN

□ **Squirmburgers & Other Tasty Tales**
0-812-54358-0 $4.99/$6.50 CAN

□ **Worm Meal & Other Creepy Tales**
0-812-54359-9 $4.99/$6.50 CAN

TOR BOOKS

"A GREAT NEW TALENT. HE BLOWS MY MIND IN A FUN WAY."
—Christopher Pike

Welcome to the PsychoZone.

Where is it? Don't bother looking for it on a map. It's not a place, but a state of mind—a twisted corridor in the brain where reality and imagination collide.

But hold on tight. Once inside the PsychoZone there's no slowing down...and no turning back.

The PsychoZone series by David Lubar

❑ **Kidzilla & Other Tales**
0-812-55880-4 $4.99/$6.50 CAN

❑ **The Witch's Monkey & Other Tales**
0-812-55881-2 $4.99/$6.50 CAN

TOR BOOKS

 Check out these titles from
Award-Winning Young Adult Author
NEAL SHUSTERMAN

Enter a world where reality takes a U-turn...

MindQuakes: Stories to Shatter Your Brain

"A promising kickoff to the series. Shusterman's mastery of suspense and satirical wit make the ludicrous fathomable and entice readers into suspending their disbelief. He repeatedly interjects plausible and even poignant moments into otherwise bizzare scenarios...[T]his all-too-brief anthology will snare even the most reluctant readers."—*Publishers Weekly*

MindStorms: Stories to Blow Your Mind

MindTwisters: Stories that Play with Your Head

And don't miss these exciting stories from Neal Shusterman:

Scorpion Shards

"A spellbinder."—*Publishers Weekly*

"Readers [will] wish for a sequel to tell more about these interesting and unusual characters."—*School Library Journal*

The Eyes of Kid Midas

"Hypnotically readable!"—*School Library Journal*

Dissidents

"An Involving read."—*Booklist*